The Light Travellers:
Luke's Journey

By Alison Cooklin

Published by Alison Cooklin
Text copyright © 2015 Alison Cooklin
All rights reserved
ISBN-13:
978-0993492013 (Alison Cooklin)
ISBN-10:
0993492010

To my husband Paul
My children Rafe and Aisha

.

CONTENTS

1
THE DROWNING

Luke would always remember the day of his drowning. He had been scaling the rocks and boulders of the cliffs near his home, scuttling like a large crab across their jagged surfaces. He never tired of treasure hunting amongst these Cornish cliffs. He was always hoping to find some kind of marine treasure, perhaps a human artefact washed up by the tides. His best find so far had been a rusted old gun, wedged hard into a crevice.

Despite his pleasure in poking amongst the rocks and their salty pools, the darkening sky had reminded him that it was getting late, time to head back home. Besides, it was getting uncomfortably cold. Chilly autumn winds whipped his straight, black hair around his face and froze his wet hands. Rubbing the gritty sand from his tanned fingers, he had scrambled down to a thin vestige of beach that was being rapidly claimed by the sea. Nearby was a small, low cave, known to very few people. At high tide it filled completely with water, but when the water line was low it made a great hiding place for his surfboard. Before he reached the cave he saw to his horror that the cave was already filling with water and his beloved surfboard was being stealthily carried away by the tide. That sleek, white board meant so much to him. He felt panic rise inside of him. He could not let the sea steal it away from him!

The board had been a year-long project, crafted by his dad and himself when his dad had felt well enough. When his dad's cancer had been in remission, Luke and his father had spent hours in the garage. They honed, smoothed and shaped the board into perfect balance. At other times, during the painful periods of his dad's treatment, the board had lain neglected and forgotten. But eventually the chemotherapy treatment seemed to have worked, his dad began slowly to recover and the board was finally finished. They decided to keep it simple in decoration, just a plain white, but with a fierce pair of eyes painted on the underside that glared at any sea creature that dared approach it. That board meant the world to Luke. And now it would be carried away to sea, if he didn't act fast.

Fighting a rising panic, Luke slithered painfully down the rocks and waded cautiously into the icy sea. He had hoped that he might be able to wade out to the board but the water was deeper than it had seemed and he realised he would have to swim out to it. Quickly pulling off his fleece and throwing it to shore Luke plunged into the water, shuddering with the cold shock. The wind pulled spitefully at his hair and hurled salty water into his gasping mouth as he swam strongly towards the surfboard. Just as his hand seemed close to the board, a great invisible weight pushed him hard under the churning water. Luke struggled in surprise and fear but try as he might, he could not seem to surface. It felt as if unseen hands were holding his legs and arms, preventing him from swimming. Luke swallowed down sea water as he wriggled to free himself but instead he sank down and down. His chest hurt, feeling crushed. He fought furiously against this unseen force that seemed determined to drown him. Then panic was clouded with darkness and all sensation faded away.

From this point his memories of the drowning became unclear. There had been light, lots of light, beginning inside his head and spreading out and around him like a warm blanket. Then he had felt gentle hands touch his limbs and his head, lightly but firmly. There was a tingling that began in his feet and seared upwards until it reached his scalp. Then he saw a burst of glorious colours, as if he were drowning inside a rainbow. Then, nothing.

As the darkness drained from his mind, Luke became aware that his body was being pushed and rocked about. He reached his arms out to steady himself and met some kind of soft resistance. He opened his eyes and had a strange feeling of being under water still.

Then he had met Keeya. How hideous she had first seemed to him! Whilst he floated there, confused and barely conscious, a distorted face had swum into his blurred vision, looking intently at him. Luke had recoiled, squeezing his eyes shut in the hope that the vision would disappear. When he opened them again a pair of huge, dark eyes stared back at him still. In contrast to the dark eyes, the eye lashes were ice white, as was the long flow of hair that drifted about the pale, bony face. As the strange face continued to stare at him, Luke saw in those alien eyes a gentleness and intelligence. Some of his fear subsided, though the face was so strange to him. It seemed to be female for there was a delicacy about the face and he noticed feminine decorations of shell combs amongst the white hair that floated around her face. Floated? It was then that Luke finally realised that he was suspended in water. Was he still drowning? He felt strange, as if lots of time had passed, though his most recent memory was of struggling to breathe.

'Did you try to drown me?' he had demanded angrily. His voice gurgled as water bubbled in his throat, yet somehow it did not choke him. He clutched first his throat, then his chest. How can I still breathe? he had thought to himself in wonder.

'I don't know. Are you one of us? Are you Eeshu?' answered a soft, girlish voice. The voice had sounded clearly in his mind but not his ears.

At first Luke had not been able to respond. He was trying to understand what was happening to him. He stared about him in amazement, realising that he was underwater and breathing normally as if he were breathing fresh air. He pressed his hands against his chest. How can this be? He swelled out his chest and had the curious sensation of cool water passing through his skin and into his lungs. It felt delicious and brought even greater clarity to his amazed mind. Again he looked at the female being who floated before him. Though her appearance was strange she no longer appeared so frightening. Her body was very long and her spine was arched, like the back of a dolphin. She was wearing a long, white robe that was tied in the middle with a cord. There was a small bag attached to that cord. He had expected to see her with a tail, believing her to be some kind of mermaid, but she had long feet clearly visible beneath the hem of her robe. Her toes were very long and flattened, like the flippers of a seal. Her arms and hands were extraordinarily long and slender, as was her neck. Her face was human in its expression, though the features were so sharp and small and the eyes unnaturally large. But it was her colouring that made her appearance so especially strange. Her skin had a greyish lustre, her enormous eyes were a dark, cobalt blue with strangely elliptical irises and her hair was long, thick and white. The only hint of warmth in her colouring was the pink tinge to her thin lips.

She smiled shyly at Luke though her face expressed puzzlement. Then she turned to look behind her, beckoning to someone. Through the gloom of the murky water another figure appeared. This time it was an elderly male, twice the length of the young female. His pale, grey face was swathed in a long, white beard and he too had the enormous, penetrating dark eyes. Luke had felt terrified of this huge male being whose expression held none of the gentleness of the female. He was reminded of images of the mythical sea god Triton. Could this be him? Luke wondered. It was all so bizarre; anything at this moment seemed possible.

Fear stimulated his drowsy, bewildered mind. Luke thought of his parents and he was overwhelmed with a need for them. They would rescue him from this strange hallucination he was experiencing. But before he could cry out for his parents he heard the voice of the sea girl, clear as crystal, speaking inside his head.

'This is my grandfather, Coryan, and I am Keeya,' said the young girl, though no words had come from her smiling mouth. The grandfather simply frowned his greeting. Also without moving his lips, the old man's deep voice thundered in Luke's head,

'Who are you? Why have you been sent to us?'

Luke opened his mouth to speak but instead he gargled on the sea water that filled his throat. He panicked for a moment, fearing he was drowning again. Then he realised he was still breathing and that his mind felt clear. When the old man's angry voice resounded in his head again, repeating the question, Luke found himself answering with his mind too.

'My name is Luke. I have no idea why I'm here, or how I got here...I don't know if I'm dreaming. Am I lying unconscious on the beach? Have I drowned? Am I dead and in a strange kind of heaven? I don't know! Mum! Dad! Help me!' Luke sobbed out the last words helplessly in his fear and bewilderment.

The old man's expression softened and he spoke more quietly,

'We don't understand either, but we know that we were meant to find you and help you.'

Luke gazed about the watery cave he saw that surrounded him.

'Where am I?'

Keeya glided forward and held his hand. Her slightly webbed fingers felt warm and had a rubbery texture. Luke shuddered involuntarily, not just from the shock of her touch but his realisation of feeling cold. Keeya spoke soothingly,

'We are by the shore where you appeared from. This is a small cave which the tide has filled and we are sheltering inside it. Do you recognise it?'

Luke looked around him, confused. It looked like the cave he had hidden his surfboard in. Now it was lit by a soft light. He had the strangest impression that the light was coming from Keeya. She then asked him,

'Are you human then? You look and dress like a human, and I have seen humans so I know. But you seem different.' She frowned as she tried to express her thoughts. 'Firstly you can breathe as we do, and your hands and feet are changing, even now.'

Luke looked down at his hands in surprise. The skin between his fingers had increased, looking a bit like the webbing on Keeya's hand. He felt both wonder and disgust.

'Are you a mermaid?' he demanded.

Keeya let out a gurgling peal of laughter. Bubbles cascaded upwards from her mouth. In laughter her face appeared much younger. She seemed to be a similar age to him, about twelve years old.

'Yes, and no,' she replied obscurely. 'We are sea people, and we call ourselves "Eeshu".' The word sounded like a rush of waves on the shore. 'However,' she continued, 'we are not like the funny myths you humans tell about us.'

Luke frowned.

'How do you know what we think of you?'

She smiled kindly at him.

'I can see the images in your head. Besides, we have been here on the Earth many thousands of years. There was a time when human spirits were closer to the natural world, long ago. Then we all lived alongside each other, sharing knowledge. Some of your kind even married with us and some Eeshu became land people. Perhaps you are a descendant?' She considered him. 'And yet you are more Eeshu than I have ever seen in a human, though you have funny little eyes and body. How old are you?'

'Twelve,' he said defensively. He felt annoyed by her description of his appearance. He was considered to be very tall for his age.

Keeya read these thoughts and feelings easily in him. She smiled.

'I am one hundred years old, almost. In the next full moon I shall be one hundred exactly, and my grandfather and I are travelling north to celebrate with family and friends. It is a very important occasion,' she announced grandly.

Luke thought her claim to be one hundred years old

ridiculous. She seemed hardly older than he was. In any case, he was distracted by the strangeness of his altered body, by the amazing circumstances he found himself in and by his concern for his family, who must be mad with worry for him. Amazing as it was to meet these sea people he really needed to get back to his family, back to normality, back to reality. How was he going to escape from this bizarre situation?

Keeya appeared to understand this. She stopped talking and instead watched him closely, concern on her face. A silence settled between them and Luke stared about him, unsure of what to do now, of how to regain his human body and escape. He was vaguely aware of the crustaceans and fish which were gathering around him. They seemed fascinated by him, the fish swimming in little shoals in front of him then at his slightest movement whisking away in a glitter of silvery scales.

In an attempt to distract him from his distress, Keeya explained to Luke,

'My little friends the fish are curious about you, Luke. They want to be sure you won't eat them.'

'Are they your pets?' he asked.

Keeya frowned slightly as she concentrated on reading his mind, seeking his meaning.

'No, we do not claim to own any creature, but every creature is our friend.'

'What, even sharks?' Luke had asked in disbelief.

'We respect sharks, and they respect us. There is room for us all in this beautiful ocean. Well, except for something that should not be here...'. Keeya's voice trailed off and Luke caught faint glimpses within her mind of a terrible and ancient reptilian face, with sharp teeth and pitiless black eyes. Luke shuddered with horror at the brief sight of it. Did such a creature exist in the seas? He was finding the ability to read another person's mind disconcerting.

Coryan returned to their shelter, surrounded in a halo of white light. Seaweed streamed between his fingers.

'Food,' he announced. He laid a heap of seaweeds on their laps. Keeya eagerly began nibbling some pink fronds, carefully selecting them from amongst a colourful mixture of plants. Some were delicately fronded, others were bulbous and lumpy. Luke looked at his own lapful of plants with distaste. Why was he even sitting here in this dark, watery cave with a pile of seaweed on his lap? He should be getting home, eating proper food. Would his mum have his dinner ready for him, wondering where he was? What about Dad? Luke couldn't bear to think of his dad's anxiety. He pictured them finding his sweater that he had left on the rocks. Had they found his surfboard? Would they think he had drowned? He could almost feel their pain. With a gesture of distress he threw his seaweed supper aside.

'I must get home! Please, can you help me get back to my family?' he pleaded.

Keeya stared anxiously at Luke, pity in her eyes, whilst Coryan frowned at him.

'Can we help him, Grandfather?' Keeya pleaded.

Coryan slowly shook his head.

'I don't know, child. This is all beyond my understanding, yet I know our role is to help this boy. If only we could have a Gathering right now, then we could know more.'

Luke anxiously interrupted.

'Please! I don't know if I've drowned or what has happened to me, but I know I'm alive now and I must get back home to my parents. They will be beside themselves, not knowing if I'm dead or missing,' Luke pleaded with them.

With a sigh Coryan said,

'Very well, we will try to take you back to the land.'

Luke saw Coryan exchange a concerned look with Keeya. Despite Luke's relief that they were going to help him get home he had a sense of his companions' misgivings. When they emerged from the quietness of the cave Luke was almost swept away by the swelling surges of water. Beyond the reach of the glowing light emitted by his companions the sea was densely black, violently stirred by stormy winds. It was early evening. Coryan and Keeya swam strongly ahead, supporting Luke's weaker body between them. He had always considered himself a strong swimmer but he was like a baby compared to these

Eeshu. He kicked his legs ineffectually, trying to move faster forward. Even so, after a short time he felt exhausted and had to give up kicking entirely. The Eeshu did not seem to feel their burden. They hauled Luke onto a submerged boulder, trying to stand in the shallower water. Coryan's mane-like hair emerged above the water but the Eeshu had to keep their faces beneath the waves to breathe. It was hard to keep steady against the bullying waves which pushed and pulled them.

Eagerly Luke tried to stand, supported by his companions. For a few moments he was able to raise his head above the water, glimpsing the rocky cliff that he had been playing on hours earlier. He gripped the boulder hard, cutting his hands on the barnacle-encrusted surface as he attempted to climb onto it. Suddenly he found himself gasping for breath. The air stung his lungs. He felt as if he were drowning. Instinctively he ducked his head back under the water, his lungs gratefully breathing in the salt water. Horror filled his mind as he gazed at Keeya's anxious face. No! I can't breathe in the air, he thought to himself in alarm. He struggled to his feet once more, head high above the water as he attempted to climb up onto the rocks. Again the outside air suffocated him. The pain in his chest was intolerable. He had almost made it to the base of the cliffs, crawling on his knees, dragging himself up the rocks. But his head and lungs gave way and he collapsed. Strong hands pulled him back into the sea. Luke gulped water down into his oxygen-starved lungs as he tried to recover. I must get home! he thought in panic. With another deep breath of seawater he clambered onto the boulder again, his head in the night air once more and holding the breath in his lungs for as long as he could bear it. He saw the criss-cross of torch beams up on the cliff top and heard voices shout out his name. He tried to answer, calling out, but the air was crushing his lungs. Again the pain in his head and chest overcame him and he collapsed, this time into darkness.

Luke had tried to keep safe in the darkness of his mind but consciousness became persistent and his traumatised mind had to face the horrible truth that he was no longer human and able to be with his mum and dad, safe at home. He closed his eyes in despair. Blindly he felt the webbing between his fingers and for the first time he became aware of the change of his skin texture too. It felt thicker and spongy and he felt less troubled by cold. Nausea filled his throat. He thought, I'm becoming more and more like them! He began to sob.

Then he heard Keeya's voice in his mind, gently calling his name. He tried to block the sound out. He felt her warm touch on his shoulder and shrunk away from her. He stared angrily at her.

'Leave me alone, you are disgusting,' he shouted with his mind, wanting to hurt her.

Keeya's huge eyes showed shock but she struggled to smile kindly at him. He felt bad for hurting her feelings but he was so unhappy he could not find it in himself to say sorry. He struggled up from the bed of kelp that he had been lying in.

'Where are we? How long have I been here?' he asked Keeya. She shrugged.

'We have taken you to another sheltered sea cave, a safe resting place for Eeshu. There was no point remaining at the cliffs. You cannot return to human life. Whilst you have been sleeping your body has been changing and you are now a creature of the sea. The night has passed, the moon is resting and soon daylight will come. Have some food and when you feel able, Grandfather and I will be waiting for you at the entrance of this cave. He has been giving great thought to your situation and thinks he may know how we might help you.'

Keeya swam away from him. Did her glow of light seem a little diminished since his harsh words towards her? Luke regretted being so mean to Keeya, but he felt too confused to apologise.

However her words had given him a spark of hope. Could they help him become human again? Was it still possible that he could return home somehow? He tried to swim after Keeya but found he could hardly stay upright, for he felt weak and giddy. His stomach angrily reminded him that he had not eaten for many hours. He looked distastefully at the seaweed salad he had been given, served this time on a large clam shell. Carefully he picked his way through this meagre meal, finding some varieties of seaweed palatable whilst others seemed bitter or too rubbery in texture. He began to crave thick slices of toast and butter, with marmalade or a boiled egg. And a hot cup of milky tea.

Thoughts of home were overpowering. He must find out what the Eeshu had to say. Leaving his bed of kelp he swam towards the cave entrance, noticing to his surprise that he could see more easily than before in the darkness of the cave, even without his luminous Eeshu companions to light the way for him.

Before he had reached the Eeshu, Luke heard a lovely, soothing sound, a musical whisper that trembled in his ears. It gently vibrated through his body. His aching heart felt slightly eased by its magic. Ahead of him he saw the mighty Coryan resting with his back against a rock, appearing pale and listless, whilst Keeya stood before her grandfather as she gently stroked the water around Coryan's body. She was holding a large crystal in one hand and the delightful music vibrated from her throat. When she became aware of Luke she stopped the lovely sound and gently touched her grandfather's shoulder. They both stared at Luke thoughtfully.

'What is that crystal for?' Luke asked Keeya, drawing closer to her. It was a single lump of rock made up of an irregular cluster of smaller, clear crystals. Each crystal had a glowing heart of greens and blues. He had never seen such a rock before.

'It is my healing crystal, we use them to mend ourselves. It is our medicine. The difference from your human medicine is that the crystals heal our spirit as well as our bodies. Here,' she said, carefully handing him the cluster of beautiful stones. Some of their glow had subsided but he still felt a tingle of warmth from them. The sensation travelled up his arm and straight into his heart. Some more of his despair left him. Reluctantly Luke handed the rock back to Keeya, who carefully hid it away in the small corded bag attached to her waist. Luke then looked curiously over to Coryan, who read the boy's thoughts before Luke could even ask a question.

'I am very old now, almost eight hundred of your human years, and Keeya helps keep this old body of mine still functioning by giving me regular healing.'

Luke blinked in disbelief. Eight hundred years old? But then as everything he had encountered since his drowning seemed incredible, why shouldn't this be true as well? Questions began to bubble up in his mind but even before he expressed them a series of images were presented to his mind, so clear and vivid. He saw a young Eeshu boy playing with dolphins, then he saw Coryan as a young man following the wake of great old sailing ships. He saw him swimming beneath huge icebergs. Luke saw Coryan pulling drowning sailors to shore, he saw him being amongst other Eeshu and with all manner of both familiar and strange sea creatures. The images were played in moments but Luke had known without a doubt that he had been given glimpses into Coryan's long life. He stared at the old man with renewed respect. This new information gave rise to more questions but before he could ask any the old man held up a commanding hand to stop him.

'Although we still do not understand the reason for your being here, nor your gradual transformation into being Eeshu, it is possible that we can teach you how to breathe again like a human.' Coryan looked steadily but not unkindly at the boy.

Luke felt a surge of hope. 'How?' he asked excitedly.

Keeya interrupted.

'Do you remember my telling you that long ago some of the Eeshu befriended land people? It was possible because, by the power of our thoughts, we Eeshu can alter our physical body. When we needed to walk and breathe on land we discovered that through meditation we are able to adapt our bodies as we need.'

'It will take a lot of training but as your body becomes more like us so you should be able to control your form and transform from Eeshu into human form,' added Coryan.

To help demonstrate this more clearly, Coryan sent images

to Luke's mind. Luke saw Keeya with her eyes closed, as if in a dream. Then he saw her body and face transforming into a dolphin. He watched her as she swam joyfully in dolphin form before changing back into Eeshu form. Next Luke saw images of Keeya gracefully emerging onto shore, walking naturally in human form.

'Wow!' Luke exclaimed excitedly. He couldn't wait to try!

'Wait, young boy!' commanded Coryan sternly. 'It is not so simple. Firstly it can take years to master that kind of mind control over your physical form, for it depends on the strength of your spirit, your sensitivity to nature and your ability to discipline your mind. Keeya is very skilful at this.' Coryan sent a proud glance towards his granddaughter, 'but we do not know what you and your body are capable of yet.'

Luke felt deflated. What if it took him years to learn? Or worse, what if he were never capable of transformation?

'We shall learn more at The Gathering in a few days' time,' said Coryan. 'We are heading northwards, to Keeya's birthplace, and many Eeshu will join us there. We always hold a special ceremony, where we contact the Wise Ones. We are sure to receive both guidance and assistance.'

Keeya had an excited gleam in her eyes at the mention of The Gathering. She swayed and dived impatiently like a playful seal.

'Luke, are you strong enough to travel? We need to leave as soon as possible if we are to get there in time.'

'Where are we going?' he asked curiously. Keeya paused in her playfulness, looking to her grandfather for a response.

'Humans call the place "The Hebrides",' explained Coryan. 'Eeshu have lived in those waters for thousands of years, though many have moved further north since due to the busy traffic of boats and trawlers. For that reason we must leave this place you call Cornwall and head out into deeper waters to avoid shorelines as much as possible. We will travel west of Ireland then northwards until we reach Scotland.'

Luke looked at Coryan, intrigued.

'How do you know all those land names, like Cornwall and

Scotland? Do you call them the same names as we do?'

Coryan gave a small smile as he shook his head.

'When you have lived on this planet as long as I have, you learn a great many things. Now, if you feel able, we will set off.'

2
THE TRANSFORMATION

Luke eagerly left the cave, his limbs feeling more powerful than during his pitiful attempt at swimming the previous night. His chest swelled with every breath of water, invigorating his mind and body. His eyesight had improved too. He found he could see more sharply into the cloudy depths. Early daylight pierced the water, illuminating a busy world of marine creatures below him whilst on the surface above came the feet and beaks of paddling and diving seabirds.

Luke admired the way Keeya and Coryan forged gracefully ahead. Though they had legs, when they swam they held their legs and feet firmly together like a powerful tail. They used their lower backs to undulate their bodies whilst their arms stretched forward like arrows, slicing through the water in front of them. They moved at a great pace, gliding effortlessly out into deeper, darker waters

To avoid any contact with humans they went deep out into the Atlantic Ocean, far west of the Irish coastline. Luke felt like an eagle, gliding across a vast landscape of hills and ravines. Sometimes he tried to swim downwards, to investigate the sea floor and explore what treasures it might hide but he found that it was so deep he could scarcely reach the seabed. When he spied an interesting shipwreck he kicked downwards and strained to reach out his hand towards the rotten mast of the buried boat. It was the deepest he had ever been. The pressure of water on his chest made his head ache so much that he began to feel dizzy and sick. Feeling terrified, Luke had struggled to rise before he became unconscious when to his great relief Coryan grasped his wrist and hauled Luke up into shallower water. Though the mighty Eeshu said nothing, Luke was sensitive to the anger of the old man and for many miles Luke swam meekly behind him, not daring to veer from their watery path.

The incident did not diminish his pleasure of his new surroundings. The sea world teemed with an extraordinary variety of creatures, rich in colour and form. There were whales, dolphins, seals, lobsters, starfish, jellyfish, and more creatures than he could name. Not only could he see further, he discovered that colours were brighter and details were sharper with his newly honed vision. Sometimes they would travel close to the shallow waters, along the more desolate parts of the coastline. Here, they would harvest the rich array of sea plants for their food. Luke admired the beautiful hues and shapes of the plants that grew like exotic flowers and shrubs, clinging to the rocks and cliff edges.

Much of the time they travelled in deeper waters. Here, in the sands that stretched endlessly beneath him, everything seemed further away and indistinct. Vague dark forms occasionally darted and moved, but otherwise there was little for him to see. Instead, he thought and wondered about his amazing situation.

One thing that intrigued Luke was the way the Eeshu communicated telepathically. He was growing accustomed to it himself. One problem with thought-communication was that it made telling lies impossible, for as soon as he sent words to Keeya, his real thoughts betrayed him. Earlier he had been thinking longingly of human food. He felt so hungry. Keeya had picked up these thoughts

'Luke, are you still hungry? Shall I ask grandfather to find us food?'

'No! I mean, no thanks, I'm not hungry.' Luke had smiled politely. He dreaded having to eat yet more seaweed. His stomach growled as images of sausage and chips played in his head.

Keeya had giggled and looked at him knowingly. She could see his true thoughts too clearly, too easily. He found that intensely annoying. On the other hand, he discovered that an advantage of telepathy was being able to speak clearly and instantly no matter how far apart you were. Conversation was an easy and comfortable thing, especially as words were further enriched with images and feelings.

Luke noticed that they were almost constantly accompanied by different shoals of fish. As soon as the Eeshu passed by, fish would change course just to travel alongside them. It was as if they were drawn to the white light that always emanated from the Eeshu. Then after a few minutes the fish would whisk away again.

'Keeya, why do fish keep following us? Have they never seen you before?'

Keeya smiled fondly at their fishy companions.

'They like our energy. Our vibrations seem to enervate them, and sometimes it can heal them.'

It was not just fish that were drawn to the Eeshu. Schools of curious dolphins would swim alongside them and squeak excitedly in their own dolphin language. Keeya could not resist leaping out of the water and diving deeply down again with them. With her arched back and graceful movements she so strongly resembled a dolphin herself that Luke remembered Keeya was able to transform herself into one.

'Could you show me how you transform into a dolphin?' Luke asked eagerly.

Keeya looked hopefully towards Coryan, but he frowned his refusal.

'It is too risky here in these coastal waters, with fishermen out and about at this time of day. Save it for our ocean journey.'

Luke felt disappointed.

'What is it like, when you change? Does it hurt? Do you think like a dolphin, or as yourself?'

Keeya sighed happily.

'I am always myself, whatever I become, but I feel differently. As a dolphin I feel such a joy and happiness, I want to leap and play in the waves for the sheer pleasure of it.'

Luke felt envious. It sounded so wonderful, so free. He yearned more than ever to learn transformation, not only to return as a human to his family but also to experience the bliss of being in dolphin form. He could feel the joy in Keeya as she remembered the experience. Then another thought struck him.

'Do you become other creatures, like sharks, or seals, or crabs?'

Keeya giggled at the idea.

'No! The reason we choose dolphin form is because, in evolutionary terms, we are very closely related. My original ancestors were dolphin-like animals, who, due to their intelligence, were created by Wise Ones into Naiads. At least I believe that is what humans called them. Sea nymphs.'

Luke frowned in concentration, reading the images in Keeya's mind. He saw wonderful, mischievous sea creatures, their bodies like dolphins but their faces full of human expression.

Keeya continued.

'Some of the naiads integrated with a race of human-like land creatures. These land creatures lived thousands of years before your ancestors evolved. The offspring of the Naiads and land creatures became known as the Eeshu. The great land race had wonderful powers and insight, which they then passed on to their Eeshu descendants. Most of the Eeshu chose to remain sea people, whilst others became fully land people.

'Who were these first land people? I've never heard of them,' Luke said dubiously.

'They gave their name to the great Atlantic Ocean, for that is the sea that engulfed their land and destroyed their civilisation. We Eeshu are some of their only surviving relatives.'

'Atlantis', breathed Luke as the name appeared clearly in his mind. He knew nothing of it really, just a lost city or land that had fallen into the sea. In fact he had only ever heard the name previously due to a fish restaurant of that name in his home town, and the story of this lost Atlantis had been told to him as a fairy story. As he remembered all this, the thought of the restaurant made his stomach gurgle. He could almost smell the freshly fried chips, crunchy with a sprinkling of salt. What he wouldn't do for some chips!

They paused at a particularly rugged, desolate area of the coastline in order to snack on some glutinous sea vegetables. Keeya was looking rather wistfully at the cliffs. She turned to Luke and said,

'There is an old story of an Eeshu girl falling in love with a sailor. They say that she had a great desire to see the land, and pulled herself onto a rock to see the cliffs, the grass, and to watch the birds in the sky. As you know, normally we cannot be seen by humans. Our vibration is too quick for your human eyes to see. But on this occasion a young sailor passed by in his small boat and saw her. He thought she was a seal and thought nothing of it but then she turned and saw him, their eyes met and in a moment they fell in love', Keeya said dreamily.

Her grandfather disagreed.

'Nonsense. It was not love which made the sailor trap her in his net, drag her to his home and make her live there as a slave, looking after his house and bearing his children. The others in his community would have nothing to do with her as they thought she was some kind of sea witch. She could not bear to leave her children so she pined away and died, longing to return to her home in the sea'.

Keeya looked a bit cross, preferring to think of the story as a romantic one. She objected,

'But many Eeshu have crossed the divide of the sea world onto the land world, and have married and lived happily as land people. We even have some descendants today still living along these coastlines. Some still have the ability to speak with their minds and they can see us. Grandfather, you have a land friend, the old man who lives in a lighthouse.'

Coryan nodded, but then added,

'But the days of land people being attuned enough to our world, to nature's spirit, are now passed. I have not heard of Eeshu mixing with land people for the last hundred years or so.'

Luke frowned.

19

'But I'm quite ordinary, nothing unusual, so why have I been turned into an Eeshu?'

Coryan was puzzled.

'You are a mystery. Humans are not spiritually evolved enough to be able to transform themselves and become Eeshu. I have never heard of it happening, not since the days of Atlantis. It must be that you are already of Eeshu descent. What do you know of your family history?'

Luke shrugged.

'Nothing really, I've never thought to ask. Mum's family have always been fishermen in Cornwall, and I'm not sure about Dad's family.'

'Maybe your grandmother was an Eeshu girl, captured by your fisherman grandfather,' exclaimed Keeya excitedly.

Luke laughed, thinking of his small, ordinary old nan. She could never have been a tall water spirit like Keeya. But still, the whole matter puzzled him. He took heart from the fact that it was possible to cross these two worlds and that surely he could return home to his family. He was now desperate to learn this transformation process. That, and to eat a decent human meal! He had been missing from home now for a whole day. It was about late afternoon yesterday that he had drowned.

The hunger inside of Luke and the relentless pace of swimming was making him feel weak and ill, so it was agreed that they would find some shelter and rest. Luke, whose spirits had been reasonably buoyant with hope during most of their journey, began to feel homesick. He followed the Eeshu dismally into another underwater cave, not looking forward to his seaweed meal. Hot chips, battered fish and buttered roll were all he could think of, yet it was torture to imagine it.

There was an anxious discussion between Keeya and Coryan, but they were able to keep their thoughts blocked from Luke and he took little interest in them. Later he wished that he had tried to understand better what was being discussed. For the moment he was so concerned with his own needs that he did not hesitate to go along with Keeya's suggestion when it was proposed to him.

'Grandfather and I are worried that you cannot yet survive on Eeshu food, so as soon as it is dark I shall transform and try to find you human food. I cannot promise that I will be successful, but we must try to keep you strong. We are just off the coastline of Scotland, and we can see the lights of a harbour, so we know there are some humans nearby. '

Luke looked at her, both surprised and excited. He longed to see her transform even more than he longed for human food. He was also aware of fear, pulsing like a dark energy from both Keeya and Coryan, and he began to wonder why they were afraid.

'Is it safe? Why are you going and not your grandfather?' Keeya smiled faintly.

'Even in human form he is very tall indeed, and would be far too noticeable. However, he will watch out for me and protect me if necessary.'

Keeya moved deeper into the cave. When Luke tried to follow her, Coryan held him back.

'She needs peace to prepare for her transformation. It takes great concentration and may take some time. However, we can help her in here. Sit.' Coryan indicated the sandy floor, but Luke was distracted by his surroundings. This was a more sophisticated dwelling than their primitive cave of yesterday. This cave was lined with shelves, some of which held books. On closer inspection he found these books to be made of thin, reed-like paper that was impervious to water. Luke opened one and found it inscribed with a dark, purple ink, though the lettering was a form of hieroglyphics and made no sense to him. Coryan gently removed the volume from Luke's grasp and guided him firmly to the centre of the cave.

Coryan then sat opposite Luke. He looked deeply into Luke's eyes and so into his mind, seeming to make some kind of assessment before leaning back and addressing Luke.

'We can help Keeya by giving some of our energy to her. It will also be a good opportunity for you to begin meditation, for without it you will never learn to transform.'

Coryan then passed a smooth, flat stone of a semitransparent, milky white into Luke's hand.

'Concentrate your mind on this stone. Try to feel the energy from it and then hold that feeling inside of you. When the energy and light have filled you, try to picture Keeya walking and breathing as a human. Keep that image in your mind for as long as you can.'

Luke closed his eyes. The stone in his hand felt smooth and pleasantly heavy. He traced his thumb over some ridges around its edges and tried to feel its energy. He was not sure what that was supposed to feel like. With a sigh he squeezed his eyes closed, straining to concentrate. 'Let go. Let go and relax.' The voice in his head was gentle but firm so he tried to relax, but his mind began to wander and his thoughts inevitably turned to Keeya. Has she changed yet? he wondered. He imagined her finding real food and his stomach churned, distracting him. This is hard work, he thought to himself in exasperation. He took a peek at Coryan and was surprised to find the old man glowing with rainbow colours. His eyes were closed and his face looked blissfully serene.

Luke closed his eyes again. A vision formed in his mind of a circle of disembodied faces beaming at him. It was like seeing a daydream, yet not a daydream that he was consciously creating with his mind. Gradually some of the faces began to form bodies, tall bodies robed with colour. He had no idea who the faces belonged to, but he could hear them calling his name. 'What do you want?' he asked them, automatically speaking with his thoughts.

'Listen to the Eeshu, study and learn, and all will be well', the gentle voices promised him. They said no more but their faces became clearer to him, both young and old, male and female. Were they angels? Luke wondered. They continued to smile benignly at him, and he felt a lovely, warm, joyful feeling fill his heart. Luke strained to see more of these beings of colour and light, but instead their forms dissolved slowly into whiteness, then faded altogether.

Luke opened his eyes, thrilled by the experience. He looked down at the stone he was clutching. Did it have magic powers then? Who were those people of light? He looked at Coryan and was disconcerted to find the old man was scrutinising him.

'What did you see?' Coryan asked him.

'I don't know', Luke answered hesitantly. Had it been just his imagination? But it had been so unexpected to see that circle of faces, how could he have made it up?

Before Luke was able to confide in Coryan, Keeya joined them, smiling a little nervously. She appeared smaller, and her spine seemed less arched, but otherwise her appearance was little changed. Luke felt disappointed. This was not the transformation he had imagined.

'She cannot fully transform until we are close to shore, or she would drown,' Coryan explained. Then he addressed his granddaughter, concern in his face.

'Are you ready, beloved?'

Keeya gave a nervous nod and all three of them set off. The Eeshu were so anxious that their mood affected Luke too and he began to feel guilty for being the cause of all this difficulty. Are they worried about being seen by humans? What is the worst that might happen, other than getting strange looks from the local people? How will Keeya buy food, do they have money to use? Why haven't I thought about this before? He chided himself for his selfishness, thinking only of his hunger and nothing of the difficulty and risks that Keeya might need to face for his sake.

It was late evening by now and the night creatures of the sea had emerged for hunting whilst the friendly shoals of fish seemed to have vanished. It was another gloomy, stormy evening which echoed their mood. They kept their minds silent, fighting through the swelling waters until they arrived at a harbour wall. Within the harbour the seabed was crowded with anchors, chains, fishermen's debris and the hulls of sheltering boats. There was a strong smell of oil, and the water felt thick and choking in their lungs. It was so strange for Luke, viewing a familiar human landscape from a completely different perspective. The picturesque harbour above seemed ugly and unnatural when viewed from beneath the waves.

The three of them found shelter beneath one of the boats, and they lingered dismally with no real plan of how to proceed. The water was so shallow that they were able to stand in the slimy mud. Luke grabbed an anchor chain then pulled himself upwards, peering just above the water whilst still breathing in the sea. The glare of lights hurt his newly sensitive eyes. He could hear shouts and laughter from a nearby pub. He found the sounds jarring. How strange that the human world should seem alien to him tonight, even hostile, yet he had happily lived as a human being all his life.

His musings were interrupted when Keeya surfaced beside him, only she was raising her whole face above the water, gasping as she struggled to cope with breathing air. He gazed at her, mesmerised by her full transformation. She still had strangely white hair and lashes and her eyes were huge in her finely boned face but her skin now appeared pink and fragile. She appeared both beautiful and strange to him. He then became aware of the torment she was in, for she gripped his arm and kicked against him as her lungs struggled to cope with the outside air. The pain in her face disturbed him. This was not the joyful transformation into human form that he had imagined, for she was clearly in agony. Keeya swooned against him, then after a few moments seemed to recover herself.

'Keeya, are you alright?" he asked her urgently. Ducking his head fully beneath the waves he scanned the churned water for Coryan, but he had disappeared. Why had Coryan gone at such a crucial moment for Keeya? Without his authoritative presence Luke felt scared and confused. He returned to Keeya, struggling to keep his eyes above the waves.

'Keeya, what are you going to do? It's too busy, people will see you. It's not worth it. And Coryan has gone, I don't know where. We should at least wait till much later, when everyone has gone to bed and it's safer to leave the sea.'

Keeya shook her head.

'Do not worry, Luke. Grandfather has gone to keep watch by the steps over there. If I stay calm and keep in the shadows, no one will bother me. This is important, for without your human food you may not survive.' She gave his arm a reassuring squeeze.

Keeya waded over to some stone steps which led up out onto the harbourside. Luke clung to the anchor chain, feeling guilty for being the cause of all this trouble and somewhat envious of Keeya's transformation to human form despite the discomfort she had had to endure. Her long sea robe fortunately looked like a slightly unusual summer dress but even so her appearance would seem odd to a human and Luke felt worried for her.

The waters within the harbour were much calmer than in the open sea but even so Luke struggled to keep his gaze above the water, for his vision was constantly blurred by foaming waves. He found the taste of the oily water disgusting too and hoped that Keeya could snatch any old crust and that they could leave here as soon as possible. If only he could see her properly. What was happening?

'Where are you, Keeya, are you OK?' His mind sent his question to her. For a moment there was silence, then she replied,

'I am on shore. Do not worry, Grandfather is watching me. I shall be back soon.' Her words sounded confident, but Luke could feel the anxiety in her thoughts.

'Good luck!' he replied back to her. Then he thought to himself, I wonder what she can get for me? Please let it be chips! Or buttered bread, or a packet of crisps. Or maybe a chocolate bar.

Luke was unable to see much, hanging onto the anchor chain and bobbing cautiously above the waves. He sat down in the dark shadows beneath the fishing boat, sliding his feet sulkily in the mud and examining his webbed hands. He was feeling disturbed by several things. Firstly, when imagining the chips or crisps or chocolate, he found they didn't seem so very appealing after all. And the thought of fish in batter made him want to be sick. He thought of fish as more than just food now. Fish in the sea were like birds in the sky, and it seemed wrong to think of them as food.

The second thing that disturbed him was the fact that he did not feel at all comfortable in this human environment. He was still longing to be with his parents and he missed his cosy bedroom, his computer and his telly, but at this moment he felt an outsider to the human world. Yet despite all the amazing new skills his body had acquired he still felt different from his Eeshu companions. In fact he felt very sorry for himself indeed. Caught in a world he could not be fully part of and now a stranger to his own world, deprived of his home and family. A huge lump formed in his throat and he wanted to cry but the tears could not seem to form. The only release was to let his sorrow shake his body. He huddled up in a ball, clutched his knees and sobbed.

'Grandfather! Help me, Grandfather!' Keeya's terrified voice cut through Luke's self-pity.

Still huddled beneath the boat Luke received images from Keeya's mind, seeing though her eyes. An ugly, distorted face jeered at her, a young man teetering unsteadily with a bottle of beer in one hand. The man was trying to grab Keeya's arm as he called out to some unseen companions,

'Will you look at this freak, she was trying to steal from us. Let's teach her a lesson.'

The last image Luke saw was of the man hitting Keeya in the face and at the same moment he felt her fear and pain before he lost all contact with her mind. Instantly Luke swam towards the harbour steps, his only thought to save Keeya. He slipped on the silted stones, struggling to stand up his haste. With a deep breath he crawled out of the water and up the steps, his lungs bursting in his chest. He heard a harsh voice shout,

'There's more of these freaks, let's get them!' and a clatter of footsteps came nearer.

'Luke, no. Swim away fast as you can!' a voice shouted in his mind. As if from nowhere, the mighty Coryan appeared carrying Keeya's limp body in his arms. Coryan leapt into the water, surging swiftly through the waves whilst clutching Keeya with one powerful arm.

Luke collapsed into the water after him, escaping the angry

shouts of their pursuers. He dived as deeply as he could. Luke felt sharp objects hitting him and he kicked away, swimming faster than ever before. He did not stop, not even to look behind him, until he had left the harbour and reached open water. He could not see his friends and he frantically called out with his thoughts,

'Coryan, where are you?'

'Nearby, Luke. Meet us at the cave. Go now, we are still not safe!' the old man told him urgently.

'What about Keeya? Is she...?'

'No, she is alive. Go!'

Luke did not dare disobey and continued onwards. He was surprised to find that he could remember the route back even without guidance. Once inside the cave he could not settle until his friends had joined him. His mind reeled at the events of the evening. Why had those people been so hostile to them? Why so vicious? How badly had they hurt Keeya? Then another thought struck him. How can she breathe beneath the sea if she is still in human form? Will she drown? Where are they?

Coryan finally returned with Keeya. She was too weak to swim by herself so her grandfather had to pull her gently along by her arms. He looked exhausted himself and he stumbled a little as he laid his granddaughter gently onto a mattress of kelp. Luke swam up beside her, anxiously examining her face. She had returned to her familiar Eeshu form but one side of her face was purple and swollen. Luke was shocked at the size of her injury. He felt sick with shame. He felt ashamed of the humans who had attacked such an innocent girl and he felt ashamed that she had suffered all this to satisfy his desire for human food.

Reading his thoughts of food, Keeya's eyes fluttered open. She fumbled weakly in her bag then drew out some yellowish lump, offering it to him with a faint smile. Dumbly Luke accepted her gift. It was a handful of squashed and disintegrating chips. He looked at it with disgust but tried to give Keeya a smile of thanks. All that distress and trauma, for the sake of that revolting mush?

From that moment on Luke was determined not only to eat like the Eeshu but to do all he could to prevent Keeya or her grandfather ever risking their lives for his sake again. He glanced over to where Keeya lay, looking peaceful despite her injury and in his heart he felt a squeeze of affection for his sea friend and all that she had done for him. He felt for the white stone that Coryan had given him and drew it out of his trouser pocket, looking at it thoughtfully. Could I use this as a healing stone too? he wondered.

Quietly Luke went to Keeya's side, holding the stone. He gazed at it, noting the way it reflected back the luminous glow from his hand. Turning his hand over in wonder, he realised now that he too could emanate his own Eeshu light. It made him feel special and more confident that he might have the power to heal. Using blind instinct rather than understanding, he brought the warm stone to just above Keeya's face and held it there, imagining the angry, purple stain fading away. The stone began to feel too hot to hold, and he looked at it in alarm. Quickly shoving the stone back in his pocket, Luke moved away, worried that he may have caused more harm than good. Keeya continued to sleep peacefully. With a sigh of exhaustion, he drifted down onto a bed of kelp to rest.

3
THE GATHERING

Daylight seeped into their shelter, bringing the promise of a happier day. Luke awoke feeling rested and keen to begin a new day of discovery. Keeya also seemed to be in high spirits. Amazingly, her face showed barely any sign of injury. Luke hoped it was because he had helped to heal her, but he felt too shy to mention it.

They made a quick breakfast. No comment was made at Luke's sudden enthusiasm for eating the sea plants. It was as if Coryan and Keeya understood that he no longer desired human food, though no one wanted to mention it. Last night was in the past and never to be discussed again. Besides, Luke found he was actually enjoying his seaweed meal. His palate was altering, just as his body and other senses were. The plants he ate each had interesting and varied flavours. Some tasted sweet, some were surprisingly spicy.

Today the sea was calm and it sparkled in the soft autumn sunlight. A group of seals joined them, keen to nudge them into play. Keeya and Luke happily obliged, chasing and diving with them. It was like being surrounded by playful dogs and Luke laughed at their cheeky antics. Their playtime was interrupted by the appearance of Coryan. Without a word, he headed for the open sea and their journey began again in earnest.

Keeya especially seemed in high spirits. Everything seemed to make her smile and laugh. It was incredible to think that it was only hours since her terrible experience on land.

'Later today we shall be home, and we shall have a wonderful Gathering, such as I have never experienced before. Oh Luke, I can't wait for you to see it, and to meet all my friends and family.'

Luke smiled at her happiness.

'What is this Gathering? Is it a family get-together, like a party?'

Keeya paused in her dolphin-like leaps in the water to consider his question.

'Yes, in that we all gather with friends and loved ones, but it is more than a party. It is rather a special birthday celebration for me too.' Here she blushed slightly. 'However, a Gathering is a special meeting with the Wise Ones. The Wise Ones give us guidance, healing and strength. It is the most blissful experience you can imagine.'

Seeing Luke's bemused expression she sent him images to explain. He saw a large number of Eeshu, of all ages and colouring, standing in two concentric circles and a small circle of four Eeshu at the centre. There was beautiful music vibrating in their throats and bright, dancing colours surrounding them. He had a sense of other beings there too, hovering above the circles, but he could not clearly see who they were.

'Who are these "Wise Ones" that you keep talking about?' he asked.

Keeya explained as well as she could.

'They are higher beings who live outside of this planet and they connect with us here in the oceans to give us the light of knowledge, love and healing. They have guided us since the Earth had conscious life on it.'

'Oh,' said Luke, nodding as if he understood. These Wise Ones sounded rather intimidating. He preferred to find out more about the other Eeshu. Keeya and Coryan had seemed so solitary. Luke had assumed they had no other family. Keeya had never even mentioned her parents. In fact Luke had never even thought to ask her, being so concerned with his own problems. He now felt consumed with curiosity about Keeya and her life.

'Where are your parents? Will they be at the Gathering?'

Keeya's face clouded suddenly, and he could feel the pain inside of her.

'My mother died when I was very small and my father died in the net of a trawler, not so long ago.'

She had her face turned away from him but Luke was conscious of her sorrow. He felt bad for spoiling her happy mood but he had no idea what to say to make it better, so they continued on for some miles in silence.

Luke reflected on what Keeya had told him. So she, too, knew what it felt like to be wrenched from your family, he realised. At least his parents were still alive. Luke pictured his mum and dad at home and sent longing thoughts to them.

'I'm alive! I'm safe and I'm alive, and soon I'll find a way to come home', he promised them. It gave him some measure of comfort, though he didn't really believe they would be able to hear his thoughts. So instead he began to think more about this great event that he was travelling to and questions teemed in his mind. He asked Keeya,

'Why are you so far from home? Where have you been?'

Keeya rolled on to her back to answer him, lazily undulating her long body as she continued to glide smoothly through the water. She smiled at him, glad to speak of happier things.

'Grandfather has taken me on a special journey, to the other oceans of the world, to learn and prepare for this celebration. You see, my hundredth year is very special to the Eeshu as I will take my place amongst the healers and spiritual leaders in our community.'

'That sounds all a bit serious and responsible. Aren't you still a child, like me?'

She looked at him a little mockingly.

'I may be a young Eeshu, but I have had a hundred years to learn about life. You humans can never achieve our level of understanding, for you don't live long enough!'

Luke frowned in annoyance, and retorted,

'Well you don't seem much older than me, so maybe you need to live a long time because it takes you so long to learn things!'

He expected her to react angrily but Keeya erupted into laughter.

'Maybe that is so', she replied, and she dived playfully around him. Suddenly she twisted and dived deeply for a few moments, then rose up alongside Luke, triumphantly holding something that trailed in her hands.

'What is that?' he asked dubiously, looking at what appeared to be some plastic rubbish.

'Your new clothes!' she answered happily.

'Clothes? But that's just some piece of human litter! Some old plastic shopping bags, I think.'

'Ah, but some human waste can be very useful, before it breaks into polluting fragments. We weave these materials to make a cloth and we use juices from plants to bind it and seal it, so that it becomes strong and flexible. See, my own dress is made this way,' and she twirled around to show him.

Luke looked more closely at her long white dress and realised he could still see faint traces of a supermarket logo but the weaving was so fine and skilful he could not believe it had begun as rubbish.

'These plastic bags are a lovely shade of blue. My friends will be able to use it to make a fine new outfit for you, more suitable than the funny garments you are wearing now.' She looked pointedly at his shrunken trousers and top and Luke followed her gaze.

It was true, his clothes did look silly, tattered and stretched now that his Eeshu form had become longer. The fabric felt heavy and restrictive but he felt some reluctance to let go of his human clothes.

They had only been travelling a few hours when several figures burst up from the depths, shouting joyously. Eeshu appeared as if from nowhere and were enthusiastically embracing Keeya and Coryan, whilst giving cheery smiles to

Luke. Luke was interested to see other Eeshu, but at the same time he felt disturbed by their noise and company. He realised how much he had enjoyed Keeya's exclusive company and now that she was being borne away by her friends and family he began to feel alone and lost.

A young male Eeshu beckoned to him to follow them, and Luke sulkily followed the bubbling trail left by the others. He was now very conscious of his human attire and wished he could feel more part of Keeya's world.

The greeting party led them close to a rocky underwater cliff, which showed above the waterline as a tiny island inhabited by sea birds. Beneath the waves the cliff spread wide like a mountain slope, thickly glued with shellfish and anemones. Everyone dived deeply down this rock face until they came to a huge open cavern beneath. It was breath-taking inside, for the sheer number of glowing Eeshu that awaited them made the cavern appear like a brightly-lit cathedral. As Luke gazed around in wonder, he realised this was not merely a single cavern, but a lofty entrance hall leading to a network of tunnels and chambers densely populated with sea people and creatures. A large purple octopus pulsed by Luke like a deflating, fleshy balloon. Crabs scuttled away like mice, fleeing into hidden corners.

Luke found himself being jostled by those trying to greet Keeya. She was beaming happily and gliding amongst her folk like a returning warrior queen. Luke felt irritated at being forgotten by her but then Coryan appeared by his side and took Luke by the arm, firmly but kindly.

'She will not forget you for long. She has been away from home for a long time, and these Eeshu love her very much. I will take you to a place where you can rest and eat, and Keeya will join you as soon as she can.'

Coryan led Luke along a labyrinth of corridors. Some opened into wide spaces, brightly lit by garlands of plants that glowed like colourful fairy lights. Seeing his wondering gaze, Coryan explained,

'Light from the sun is absorbed by the plants, and the plants convert some of that energy into their own light.'

Each wide open space was like a town square and the corridors that intersected them were like streets. The high rocky walls of each square were studded with cosy looking caves, some several stories high. These cave homes were large and well furnished. Many were surrounded with lush vegetation that clung to the rock faces like hanging gardens. Bright shoals of fish swarmed like butterflies amongst the plants.

Peeping discreetly inside these cave homes, Luke could see curious faces looking back at him. Some Eeshu smiled and waved at him but most nodded reverently towards Coryan as he moved majestically past them.

'What do you call this place?' asked Luke.

Coryan shrugged.

'We do not name our communities, as there is no reason for it. We can read each other's minds and hearts to know where and what a place is.'

Coryan drew up to a large, magnificently furnished cave. Smoothly chiselled walls were lined with fine mother of pearl and thinly sliced crystals. It glittered so brightly that Luke had to blink his light-sensitive eyes as they entered. The entrance room, open to the street as all the other homes had been, was furnished with exquisite marble tables and chairs. There were statues and ornaments carved from solid rock crystals and plates, bowls and cutlery wrought from a gleaming metal, perhaps a fine gold or platinum. It looked like the palace of a king and the scale and sophistication of the room took Luke's breath away. He had thought Eeshu were simple, nomadic folk but this complex underwater city, with all its fine decoration, lighting and furniture made him realised the Eeshu were far more sophisticated than he had realised. Coryan, imposing as always, looked more God-like than ever amidst this splendour

An old Eeshu lady emerged from a chamber which led off from the entrance room. After greeting her fondly, Coryan then turned to Luke and said kindly,

'Go with Gurrya, she will look after you until it is time for the Gathering.'

Coryan then joined a group of Eeshu who were waiting patiently outside his home. Luke allowed himself to be gently guided by the elderly Eeshu lady into a large bed chamber, where a deep bowl-shaped bed dominated the room. The bed was made of a pearly shell that was so fine that the light glowed through it. Luke wanted to flop wearily onto the bed but was conscious of the Eeshu lady beside him. She was friendly but rather shy with him and apart from asking simple questions such as, Was he hungry? Would he like to rest? she soon left him to himself.

Luke absently nibbled some food as he looked around him. It was in truth a relief to be left alone, to take stock and consider his feelings. He had become so dependent on Coryan and Keeya since his drowning that he felt bereft without them. Also, although this underwater city was fascinating, it made him feel more lost and alone than ever before. He remembered again his despair, last night in the harbour, when he had sobbed over his predicament of being neither human nor Eeshu. Self-pity threatened to weaken him again. Instinctively, he sought comfort from the magic stone that lay in his pocket. He smoothed his thumb over its familiar ridges and flaws. Warmth tingled slowly along his thumb and up into his arm. He closed his eyes, concentrating on the feeling. A soft voice whispered in his head, 'think happy thoughts', and he settled down onto the bed, lay back and tried to think of what had made him feel happy recently. His first memory was of playing with the seals, revelling in his new dexterity in the water, and sharing laughter with Keeya. He felt a smile spread across his face. Darker thoughts of his lost home and grieving parents tried to creep into his mind but he gripped his magic stone tightly and stubbornly clung to more cheerful thoughts. He remembered Keeya, soaring through the water like a dolphin. He imagined how wonderful it would feel. As he did so he could feel his own body wanting to soar above the waves, just as his heart soared and dived happily inside his body. Then the mysterious faces of the Wise Ones began to appear in his mind and he welcomed them into his thoughts, hoping to feel the calm and happiness that their contact brought to him. A voice jarred him from his meditation.

'Luke, I am sorry, but I have been sent to bring you these and to take you to join Keeya at the Gathering.'

Annoyed, Luke opened his eyes to find a tall Eeshu boy standing before him. He had the same long, ice-white hair as Keeya but it was tied back from his face and his brows were heavier and more masculine. The stranger smiled easily at Luke and introduced himself.

'My name is Biblyan, cousin of Keeya and one of Coryan's many grandchildren. Grandfather sent me with these new clothes for you and has asked me to be your guide for the Gathering.'

Luke looked suspiciously at the garments that were draped across Biblyan's arms. He disliked being torn from his happy thoughts and felt annoyed at being caught off guard. He had forgotten however that his thoughts were like spoken words and Biblyan immediately understood how Luke was feeling. He did not seem offended at all but instead laid the new clothes carefully on the bed for Luke to see.

Luke found it hard to believe that the fine robe and loose trousers that lay before him had been fashioned from plastic debris. The cloth was supple and soft and a thin metal thread had been woven into the cloth to create a subtle pattern of geometric shapes. Rather shyly, Luke struggled out of his trousers and top, exchanging them for the new robe and trousers. The fabric fell gently in folds about him, swayed by the water around them. It felt light and yet warm. Luke felt so comfortable, even though it was strange to have his legs free from restriction. Biblyan respectfully tied a small bag around Luke's waist with a long, broad band. The bag felt heavy with an object and Luke put his hand inside. He drew out a beautiful, sheathed knife. The handle was of a hard, glossy, black stone inlaid with tiny mother-of-pearl dolphins. Luke slowly examined it with murmurs of admiration.

'It is a welcome gift from me,' explained Biblyan cheerfully. 'We always carry a few essential items with us. We carry a tool like that for harvesting food, carving useful objects, protection, all sorts of things really. And we always carry a healing stone, plus a few personal items if we so choose.'

Luke felt touched by the lovely gift from Biblyan and began to feel churlish for his unfriendliness towards the boy. He looked gravely at him.

'Thank you. I'm sorry..,' he began to apologise for his behaviour when Biblyan cut him short with a dismissive gesture.

'Do not worry, it must be very disconcerting, being thrust into an unknown world and meeting strangers. Besides, I am very pleased indeed to meet you. Keeya has told us much about you already and she seems to think you are something special.'

Luke blushed with pleasure to hear that Keeya thought him special. His sense of loneliness and abandonment had now left him and he began to feel a renewed interest in his surroundings. Just as they went to leave, however, he suddenly remembered something important. Dashing over to his discarded trousers, Luke drew out his own healing stone and put it carefully in his waist bag, patting it happily.

As he followed Biblyan through the network of streets and dwellings, Luke tried not to stare too obviously at the Eeshu, seated in their open-fronted homes. He looked away awkwardly when anyone nodded or smiled at him. But after a while he began to realise there was no embarrassment to be felt, for the Eeshu enjoyed the company of passers-by. This was why they had their front room always open to friends and acquaintances. Luke compared it with the way he lived in the human world, closed in and private. That people could leave their treasures openly here for anyone to see or touch must surely mean they had no worries about thieves or trespassers. The friendliness that the Eeshu showed towards him was heart-warming and, feeling more Eeshu-like in his new clothes, Luke began to relax and enjoy himself.

'Biblyan, can you tell me about this place? How long has this city been here?'

Biblyan shrugged.

'It has existed as a home to the Northern Eeshu for thousands of years, long before the surrounding islands were inhabited by humans.'

They had arrived at a large square. It was busy with Eeshu of every hue and size. They all held small bags, plants and other objects and were patiently waiting to be seen to by an elderly Eeshu. He was making notes and labelling the objects that they gave to him. Biblyan explained,

'Eeshu from all over the world come here, bringing samples of endangered plants and animal species from their regions. The archivist then catalogues the seed and plant samples which are kept in stock, ready for replanting. With the animal species, they record their essence so they can be recreated if they become extinct.'

Luke was amazed.

'Wow, I think human scientists are doing something like that with plant species. Isn't it funny how alike humans and Eeshu can be?'

Biblyan sighed.

'Yes, but the difference between us is that we are not the ones killing these species, you humans are with your pollution and over-fishing'

Luke fell into a hurt silence, resenting both the criticism of human beings and of being considered still a human. Which he was of course, except his body was almost entirely Eeshu. Oh, it was too confusing. Luke felt a surge of anger and despair at his predicament. Of course his emotions spoke loudly to Biblyan, who looked at him pityingly.

'You know, the thing that causes you despair, this being part-human, part-Eeshu, is what makes you so very special. Coryan thinks you are vital to both our worlds.'

His words brought little comfort to Luke. Instead, Luke gazed at the variety of Eeshu that he saw around him. Curiosity overcame his unhappiness and he felt compelled to ask Biblyan more about the beings that he saw around him.

'Who are those enormous, purple-coloured Eeshu over there? They look so scary.'

Luke pointed to a group of Eeshu who towered above the others. Their skin was dark purple, they had long, ghoulish, dark hair and large black eyes. They had such a solemn and mournful appearance that Luke felt afraid of them. As if they could hear his thoughts, one such creature turned his head and fixed his black, searching gaze upon Luke. A soft, deep voice reverberated in Luke's head.

'Greetings, land-child. Take care, for you are about to face great dangers. Be safe.'

The words chilled Luke to the bone. That sounded like a threat.

Biblyan however nodded respectfully at the dark creatures and explained,

'Those are the Deep Eeshu. They live far down in the oceans, deeper than many Eeshu can survive. It is a great honour for them to come so near to the surface. They possess an ancient knowledge of our race and origins and command great respect amongst us.'

Despite himself, Luke felt intrigued.

'And what about the other Eeshu races? What about the pink and red Eeshu over there?' he asked, pointing to a troupe of smiling Eeshu who were of small and slight build. Their skin was salmon-pink and their rust-red hair streamed out like anemones.

'Coral Eeshu. You can tell the sort of environment we dwell in by our colouring. Over the centuries we have become so attuned to our surroundings that we merge with them. For example, those with the green hair and brown skin live in the muddier river estuaries, the pale yellow Eeshu with the turquoise eyes live in sandier, tropical shallows and those that live in the Arctic seas are almost completely white save for their pale blue eyes.

Luke looked carefully at his guide. Biblyan, just like Keeya and Coryan, had bluish skin, white hair and dark, cobalt eyes. Biblyan laughed as he understood Luke's thoughts.

'We are Northern Eeshu, so we reflect both icy and milder seas. As for you Luke, you are becoming almost Northern, except for those land-green eyes of yours. Keeya loves the colour of them.'

Again Luke blushed to hear kind words from Keeya. Which reminded him of her.

'Where is Keeya? I want to see her.'

'Of course, she is waiting for you to join her. It has just taken some time for her to prepare for the Gathering. You will love it. We have not had a Gathering on this scale for many years and everyone here is excited beyond bearing. And wait till you see the food, even a land-boy will love it.'

'Will you stop calling me "land-boy" please! It makes me feel, well, an outsider and I don't like it', Luke said crossly.

'Of course, Luke.' Biblyan remained cheerful as he led Luke back to the enormous entrance cavern. The place had been transformed into a banqueting hall. There was a huge circular table which could seat hundreds and at the centre was a platform on which a nervous, giggling crowd of Eeshu children stood. Luke was strongly reminded of his own school performances and smiled to see such a familiar scenario, even if the participants were worlds apart.

'Luke, how wonderfully Eeshu you look!' exclaimed Keeya as she burst away from an entourage of Eeshu women. She gave Luke a warm squeeze on his shoulder as she admired his new clothes.

Luke, however, was speechless. Keeya had been transformed into some goddess being. Luke's thoughts instantly spoke to her and she smiled at his admiration. Her robe was entirely of silver and gold, sewn with pearls of purest white, pink and smoky grey. Around her long waist was a wide, jewel-encrusted belt that reached up to her rib cage. On Keeya's chest lay an enormous emerald pendant and around her throat she wore a choker of blue stones. Across her brow lay a single gem of dark blue and upon her intricately braided hair she wore a crown of diamonds and amethysts. She looked truly majestic.

Finally, Luke was able to express himself.

'Wow, Keeya, you look like a princess!'

Biblyan looked at him in surprise.

'She is, did you not know?'

Luke's face fell.

'No, I didn't', he said quietly, though his hurt was loud and clear.

Keeya took his hand and looked deeply into his face.

'That is because being a princess, or whatever you human beings may term it, is only important here in my community, because of the role I serve here. When I am with you I am simply Keeya, your friend. That is all that matters between us.'

Luke felt somewhat mollified by her words. Some Eeshu ladies came to gently guide Keeya away. Luke allowed Biblyan to lead him to a seat at the table, which was now covered with platters of food, enough to feed the hundreds gathering around them. The noise was intensifying as the cavern filled with excited Eeshu and Luke struggled to tune out the thoughts, images and emotions that his mind was picking up from the hundreds of minds around him.

'Look inside you', whispered a voice, so soft, yet clearer than any other in his head. Luke tried to obey. Even the act of trying to look inside his own head blocked out much of the extraneous noise and he began to feel calmer.

The Gathering was opened by the children who stood on the central platform. As soon as the first piercing notes quivered from their crystal instruments the whole atmosphere changed. A hush fell over the assembly. The choir hummed a haunting melody and the water trembled around the audience with its vibration. Luke closed his eyes in order to concentrate on the magical sounds. The music not only vibrated in his ears, it could be felt as tiny ripples across his skin. Luke shivered. The music stirred powerful emotions inside him. One moment he felt tearful and despairing, the next he quivered with excitement. It was almost unbearable.

Biblyan whispered to Luke,

'Can you hear the colours?'

Luke thought he had misheard. How can you hear colours? But as he allowed the notes to pierce his heart he sensed a stream of colours. High notes swam in his mind as beautiful blues and purples, whilst the lower notes played as reds, oranges and yellows, reverberating in his belly. He felt saturated with colour.

The music softly began to drift away and its magic spell was broken. Coryan then stood at the centre, addressing the crowds with a welcoming speech as the little Eeshu scrambled off stage to sit with families. Then the feasting began. Although most Eeshu relished the rich array of prepared sea plants, Luke was horrified to see that some Eeshu were eating fish. It seemed barbaric, which was odd considering a few days ago some battered fish would have seemed delicious to Luke. Reading his thoughts, Biblyan explained,

'In some parts of the ocean, such as the depths or extreme north, there is little vegetation and the Eeshu there must survive on the creatures that live amongst them.'

When the feasting had finished, Coryan stood at the centre and hummed a single, deep note that made Luke shiver inside. Keeya took her place beside her grandfather. Her pure, high voice mingled with the deep, masculine vibrations of her grandfather's voice. Another voice joined the melody, then another and soon everyone was singing together.

At first Luke was uncomfortable with the turbulent emotions that the music stirred inside of him. He wanted to cry. His heart yearned for his family. Then just as it was becoming unbearable and he thought his heart would shatter inside him, a warmth spread through him like warm and loving arms. It melted the sadness into calm. Gradually he found his own voice vibrating the water around him. Not only did it soothe him, it also gave him a sense of unity with the souls around him. As the music swelled and rippled over his skin, Luke thought lovingly but happily of his parents. He looked at Keeya, Coryan, Biblyan and all the Eeshu who had shown him welcome and kindness, and Luke's heart expanded with affection for them all.

Now Coryan, Keeya and two elderly Eeshu took the centre stage. They each held a crystal, holding the stones up high as they radiated thoughts into them. Images of the oceans were projected onto the water in front of the audience. Luke realised they were sending healing to their watery world. One by one each member of the audience held their own crystals up. Everyone seemed intent on the same purpose, to heal and balance their world.

Next, the assembly sat down and, a few at a time, elderly and sick Eeshu made their way to the centre for some healing. A ball of light sparkled above the central group. As Luke stared, this ball of energy stretched and flickered to form bodies. These ghostly figures, the mysterious Wise Ones, hovered over the sick Eeshu below. It was interesting to watch but Luke felt very much a spectator until, to his surprise, he was led to the centre. The heat and energy crackled around him like electricity.

Keeya winked and smiled at Luke and he felt slightly less tense but even so, it was an alarming experience, suddenly being at the centre of this energy. He closed his eyes and felt a heat and pressure on his limbs. They twitched uncontrollably. His body felt electrified. It lasted mere moments, but when the pressure had passed he felt irreversibly changed inside. Cautiously Luke opened his eyes again. Above him he saw the circle of floating figures. The light that shone from them blinded him to their features. Slowly they faded away.

Feeling dazed, Luke looked over at Keeya. She smiled at him. Luke smiled back, feeling strangely at peace. He had no idea what had just happened to him. Keeya came close to him and gripped his hands, her eyes sparkling with excitement.

'Luke, we have been told that you are a light traveller. Now it all makes sense, why you have been chosen.'

Luke frowned in puzzlement. 'What is a light traveller? And what have I been chosen to do?'

'A light traveller has the ability to cross worlds, planets, even time. And you have been chosen to save our oceans. Oh Luke, I knew you were special!'

Luke felt faint. He was overwhelmed by the evening's events and felt frightened at the idea of being a chosen one, a saviour of oceans. And a light traveller? What did it all mean?

4
TO THE NORTH

The following morning nothing more was said about light travelling and saving the world. Luke was relieved. Instead he spent his time exploring the Eeshu city, learning about the Eeshu community and their way of life. It struck him how strange it was that if he were at home right now he would have been at school with his friends and classmates. They would have been talking about surfing, football, gaming and other normal, human-child activities. Luke remembered his human world as if it were all a dream rather than a reality. Life with the Eeshu had become his new reality.

Keeya was kept very busy with family and friends, so for the next few days Biblyan remained Luke's main companion. Biblyan took him beyond the safety of the island city and out into the waters of the Outer Hebrides. Luke was swimming alongside Biblyan, listening to the Eeshu boy's knowledge and understanding of the creatures and plants that they passed, when overhead there came the thunder of a boat engine. Luke froze, unsure of what to do. Biblyan gripped his hand and pulled Luke away, just in time, as a net was cast wide into the sea. Luke watched in sorrow as a startled shoal of fish found themselves ensnared. Biblyan led Luke to a crop of rocks where they could watch in safety. Luke looked curiously at his companion.

'How do you feel about human beings fishing, taking your friends out of the sea?'

Biblyan shrugged.

'Humans need to eat. Their bodies are not as evolved as Eeshu, so they rely on a primitive diet. Besides, fish are eaten by other creatures too, like seals, birds and dolphins. It is part of the balance of this world that we live in. Anyway, Eeshu have for many years been close to the fisherfolk, some may even have Eeshu ancestors.'

'Really? Keeya has told me about Eeshu and human beings mixing, a long time ago. It's hard to imagine that happening now. My friends would freak out if they saw you.'

Biblyan gave Luke a broad smile.

'I can show you how things used to be. Follow me!' he said.

Checking that they were clear of the fishing nets, they swam swiftly away, dipping down underwater gullies, soaring up rock faces and grabbing handfuls of juicy seaweed to snack on as they passed. Luke struggled a little to keep pace and was soon breathless but he was aware that his body was stronger and faster than ever before and he just managed to keep his guide in sight. Besides, it was such a wonderful morning for speeding through this beautiful underwater world.

Eventually they reached a sheer cliff which rose straight upwards, towering out of the sea and hundreds of metres into the blue sky above. It was part of another rocky outcrop, too small and barren for human habitation. They dived steeply down and came to the opening of a small cave in the base of the island rock. The boys entered, relying on their Eeshu glow to light up this gloomy place.

The walls were painted with primitive pictures, some of familiar sea creatures, some of prehistoric monsters. Luke was surprised to see crudely drawn images of trees, birds and animals. Even more surprisingly, he saw drawings of what seemed to be primitive flying machines and plans of temples or similar buildings.

'These are land things! Who drew them?' he asked Biblyan in amazement.

Biblyan shook his head.

'I do not know. They are thousands of years old. The paintings may have been drawn by ancient Eeshu. They once had a close link with land people.' He then shivered. 'This place is still filled with the energies of the people that used to live here. It makes me feel very uncomfortable. Let us get out of here, for I have something else to show you.'

The boys swooped down to the sandy seabed and strolled along it, past the debris of an old boat wreck. Biblyan pointed out the occasional discarded Eeshu artefact, shell bowls and broken pots, which poked out from the sand. They now stood a few hundred yards from a tiny cove. In front of them loomed a giant stone circle of black rocks, set deep into the sandy bed. It was composed of about thirty stones, tall and narrow and several metres high. Some were damaged and dislodged and there were gaps between them as if other stones had once stood there. All the stones were studded with barnacles and shell fish. As Luke drew closer he saw that the stones had faint traces of hieroglyphics. It was just like the writing he had seen before, in the books at the cave shelter. Full of curiosity he made his way to the centre of the ring. Luke felt strangely uncomfortable, as if the giant stones were tall people, judging him. They emitted an energy that made him tingle. As he stood there he began to see faces appearing around him, though not the angelic faces of the Wise Ones. These were primitive Eeshu faces, ancient and chilling. In horror Luke fled the circle and joined Biblyan, who was watching him from outside the circle. Biblyan laughed.

'Met the ancestors, did you? Their energy is still held in the rocks and it can be pretty scary facing them. They mean no harm, but still, we tend to avoid this place, even though it is a sacred place too. Now, I have something else to show you. Come on.'

Thankfully Luke left the haunted circle and followed Biblyan to the base cliffs of a much larger island. Biblyan then turned to Luke and asked, 'Can you transform?'

Luke sadly shook his head.

'Have you really tried? Go on, you were born a human, so breathing the air was natural to you once. Just close your eyes and imagine taking big breaths of air. Imagine it filling your lungs and feeling natural and comfortable. We shall do it together.'

The cheerful optimism of the Eeshu boy filled Luke with courage and hope. Luke closed his eyes and tried to concentrate, instinctively feeling for his magic stone and taking comfort from it. It was hard to imagine breathing air when your lungs are happily filled with seawater. Luke called on memories of walks with his father. He pictured them enjoying the vigorous coastal winds which swelled their lungs and whipped about their faces. Just thinking of his father caused Luke a pang of longing to see him. It also made him determined to get back to his dad as soon as he could. He nodded to Biblyan, indicating he was ready. Biblyan looked pleased.

'Shall we try? We shall just rise above the water for a few breaths and see how it goes, do not worry', said Biblyan reassuringly.

Together they pulled themselves up onto a rock. Luke felt the cold outside air like a slap across his face. He tried to imagine breathing it in and at first his lungs rebelled.

'Calm, Luke, relax and breathe', whispered a voice inside him. Luke tried. For a few breaths it seemed to work. Sea water bubbled in his lungs as his nostrils filled with air and drew it down into his chest. Air and water met inside him and battled for dominance, but Luke persevered. For a while it seemed to work, then his head began to spin with lack of oxygen and he sank down into the water, gasping to recover.

Biblyan was watching him carefully, but Luke nodded to him to show he was OK, though too out of breath to speak. Although Luke had not been able to transform, for a while he had been able to accept air and this was so much more than he had previously thought possible. It made him excited. If I practice this lots more, I can do this, he told himself.

'We cannot go ashore then, but we will swim over to a nearby bay and just look above the water for a few moments, so that you can see something special,' said Biblyan.

The boys swam round to the rocky edge of a wide, calm bay. They listened cautiously for any human sounds but all seemed quiet above the water, so they pulled themselves up onto a flat rock and stared out across a flat, grassy plain. Luke was astonished, but had to dive down, take more breaths then come up again to get a more detailed look. The grassy plain had a giant circle of standing stones, exactly like the circle Biblyan had shown him earlier beneath the waves. They were even of a similar shape and rock-type, and in the distance he could see another smaller ring of stones set in the ground beyond the first and larger circle.

'What is this place? Why are the stones here? What did they use them for?' asked Luke.

Biblyan looked at him in surprise.

'For holding Gatherings, of course. These rocks were blasted millions of years ago from the core of the earth. They still hold such energy that it amplifies every vibration we create. Being in a circle formation increases their power. Humans call this place "Calanais".'

The boys slithered down back into the water and Luke exclaimed,

'If only I could tell the human world about this, I bet there are lots of archaeologists scratching their heads and wondering how this was built.'

Biblyan smiled.

'Maybe you can tell them, one day. The land people that built this were close with Eeshu and their priest or priestess would have been of the sea. Grandfather said that Eeshu helped bring these rocks here. The rocks were carved by the Eeshu then floated here on rafts. The humans then hauled the rafts in their nets and landed them on shore. We used to work very closely together and both our worlds were the better for it. Our world in the sea was mirrored by the world on land. Unfortunately over time that connection has been broken. The land people became more inward looking and disconnected with nature and the sea.'

Biblyan then looked wistfully to the shore.

'Even so, it would be wonderful to experience living on the land and in the air, regaining our former connection.'

Biblyan became lost in thought and Luke could feel a deep sorrow emanating from the Eeshu boy. Biblyan carefully kept his mind closed, preventing Luke from understanding the cause of his sadness. Biblyan then turned to Luke.

'You are so lucky, you know what it is to live in both our worlds.'

Luke did not respond. He certainly did not feel lucky. However, since his drowning the Eeshu had revealed an amazing world to him that he had never dreamt existed. He had made friendships that were beginning to mean a great deal to him. In fact, Luke really had no idea of how he felt about his circumstances anymore. There were even moments when he forgot where he came from, he felt so immersed in Eeshu life. But then memories of his home and family would return to wrench him apart again.

On their return to the city, the boys were informed by Coryan that Luke was due to travel once more, this time on a much longer and more challenging journey. Luke was told more about it after the evening meal, where they had been joined by Coryan's family and some city elders. After the meal had finished Coryan turned to Luke and said,

'Tomorrow we must leave and head north, to the Arctic seas, before they freeze completely. Winter is quickly approaching.'

Luke was surprised. He thought he was to remain here, to learn the Eeshu ways, until he was ready to learn transformation. The thought of leaving this friendly and familiar environment was upsetting.

'Why must we travel at all?' he asked petulantly.

Coryan frowned at Luke.

'Because during the Gathering we were told by the Wise Ones that you must first visit the North, to bathe in the solar lights. Then we must proceed across the mighty Atlantic to Bermuda, where the prophet and prophetess live. They will help you to find the answers to your situation.'

Luke was bewildered.

'Who are the prophet and prophetess?'

It was Bibliyan who interrupted.

'Tiyan and Merya. They are my parents. They are the current spiritual guides of all Eeshu. At the moment they are on retreat and live far away from other Eeshu communities. They link with the highest vibration of all. They will be able to answer anything you need to know.'

Luke looked eagerly at his friend.

'Will you be coming with us too, then?'

Biblyan shook his head sadly. Then, seeing Luke's disappointment, he added,

'But I will come with you as far as the Faroe Islands. We have several communities of Eeshu there and I have family to visit, so I can at least begin with you on your journey.'

Luke looked down, shuddering at the thought of going into unknown, icy seas. He felt sad at the idea of leaving his friend. Luke looked towards Coryan.

'So who will be coming with me?'

Keeya, who had been watching anxiously, now broke in,

'You will be with Grandfather and me, just as before. It will be an adventure together and I am sure you will enjoy it, we all will. And just think, by the end of it we will finally be able to understand why you came to us and how to return you to your own world. That is what you want, isn't it?'

All the Eeshu looked at him and Luke mutely nodded his agreement but as ever his turbulent feelings rang out loud and clear to all those assembled there. Much as he loved the idea of spending time with Keeya, he wasn't sure he wanted to face a long journey in freezing waters. His life had been turned upside down and for now he just wanted to remain in this happy place, with his new friends. He wanted to feel some stability for a while. But he also realised that unless he did as he was told, he would never break free from his internal struggle with homesickness and the question of which world he was a part of.

The next morning, the travellers left the comfort of the city and set off across a stormy sea. The watery world seemed angry and upset that day. It mirrored exactly the way Luke was feeling. Despite Keeya's attempts at cheeriness a gloomy cloud seemed to follow them and even the chatty Biblyan seemed more withdrawn than normal. Visibility was poor as particles from the sea floor were churned around them, like a sand storm in the desert. The group maintained a silence as they forged through the turbulence with gritted teeth, each absorbed in their own thoughts. It was late in the day when they approached the first rocky islet that formed part of the Faroe Islands. Luke was shivering with cold. Since the Gathering, Luke was aware that his body had completed its transformation into becoming Eeshu. He could swim strongly, he could see for miles and he could cope with freezing temperatures that would have killed him in his human form. Even so, he was not as hardy as his companions and the misery of feeling so cold darkened his mood even more.

Keeya, Coryan and Biblyan on the other hand seemed to cheer up at the sight of the underwater cliffs ahead of them. Before long, more Eeshu came to join them, welcoming them all enthusiastically and leading them to a small but cosy cave network buried deep beneath the islet. It was toasty-warm inside thanks to volcanic activity, deep below the roots of the islet. Luke began to feel more cheerful as his cold and aching limbs began to thaw.

They had scarcely begun to rest when an Eeshu girl came rushing in, wringing her hands in anxiety.

'There are souls to rescue! Follow me. Four fishermen are drowning nearby, we must be quick!'

In an instant all the Eeshu present became alert. With grim determination they surged after her. Luke felt obliged to follow too, though he felt weary from the effort of his journey. He soon found himself back out in the angry sea. It was even more ferocious than before. He had to battle against it to keep the others in sight.

Human cries rang in his ears. Even before he reached the wreck of the boat he could see the terrified faces of the grizzled and bearded fishermen clearly in his mind. As he reached the scene he saw that the Eeshu were supporting four of the men, all of whom had slumped into unconsciousness. Biblyan swam up to Luke and explained,

'We have to make them unconscious, for if they feel us holding them they panic and struggle and it makes it so much harder to help them.'

Luke could keenly remember his own terror at his drowning and the unseen hands which had deliberately pulled him under. Had that been Eeshu hands, drowning him? Keeya and Coryan had denied that they had done it. They said they had been guided to save him. So who had drowned him? Luke felt both angry and helpless for having had his life deliberately changed in this way by unseen forces.

Luke was distracted from his thoughts by another human cry of terror. He turned to see a man clawing helplessly in the water, gulping and flailing. Luke and Biblyan shot forward, trying to help the man but Coryan stopped them and held Luke back. Two Eeshu now held the drowning man and by placing their hands on his brow they appeared to relax him into sleep. Luke felt relieved, thinking the man was about to be carried to shore with his fellow sailors, when to his horror he saw the Eeshu gently release the man's body and let it sink slowly to the bottom.

'No! You've killed him! Why?' Luke tried to capture the body as it sank but Coryan held him back firmly.

'Luke, wait! It is the man's time to die. It is why we are here, not just to save lives but to help others to die as gently as possible. Watch and see, his soul is alive still.'

Luke struggled against Coryan's restraining arms but then saw a shimmering light above the lifeless body of the sailor. A rainbow stream of colours drifted upwards and then began to settle into the recognisable form of the drowned man. The man's spirit seemed sleepy and confused as he looked around at the Eeshu faces smiling at him. Coryan came forward, took the man's hand and began communicating privately with him. Slowly understanding spread across the man's face. The fisherman looked upwards at an unseen presence above him, offered his hand with a happy smile and was slowly drawn away from sight.

Luke was dumbfounded. Was that death? Had the man's spirit been taken to heaven? Luke looked down at the limp corpse, lying crumpled on the seabed like a pile of old clothes. He realised it was no more than debris, that nothing of the man remained there. Luke found that he didn't feel sad at all. The man's spirit had seemed happy and peaceful, yet somehow still vital, as in life.

Coryan had been watching Luke carefully and he put a comforting arm across the boy's shoulder.

'Death is not a terrible thing, it is not the end. In fact, it is a wonderful new beginning. Do not feel sad for that soul, for he was happy to leave this world. It was his chosen time to do so.'

'But why did he drown and not the others? How did you know who to save and who to let go?'

Luke felt disturbed that such a momentous choice had been made by these Eeshu but Coryan understood Luke's thoughts and shook his great head.

'We knew, because even before we reached the boat wreck, the Wise Ones had told us what would happen. We knew there were four souls to remain on Earth and one to pass on. And when we reached this place, we could see the friends and relatives of the man who was drowning, waiting for him to join with them. He was happy to go. Death can be a beautiful thing.'

Luke imagined his parents, mourning his loss. He knew they would think him lost and drowned, like that fisherman and he pictured their agony. He shook his head, aching for them and longing to tell them he was alive.

'Luke, I know you hurt for your family and I can understand because I have lost loved ones too. But if you practice your meditation and ask the Wise Ones for help, I am sure they can send hope to your parents, to let them know you are not entirely lost to them. Come back with me, to the home of my friends, and we will all meditate with you. Perhaps we can reach your parents through their dreams.'

A week ago Luke would have thought this a hopeless quest but each day brought him a deeper understanding. He had a wonderful sense of the spirit and light which stitched the layers of their worlds together with invisible thread. He knew there was a good chance that he could in some way communicate with his family.

With his tired mind reeling with all that he had just seen, Luke followed the Eeshu back to their warm and welcoming homes. After a pleasant meal, their Eeshu hosts moved the furniture into a circular formation, ready to hold a small Gathering. There was a simmering excitement inside of Luke. He was hoping to connect somehow with his parents. A hush fell and the Eeshu closed their eyes, settling comfortably within their own minds. Luke closed his eyes and tried to breathe deeply, to relax, just as Biblyan and Keeya had been training him to do. Before long he began to see the familiar faces of the Wise Ones appear in his mind. Help me! he asked them. A clear image of his parents appeared in front of him, looking befuddled with sleep. It was bittersweet for Luke to see them. It was wonderful to see their familiar, careworn and beloved faces but it pierced his heart not to be able to hug them. His mind called out to them,

'I'm alive! Don't give up on me! I'm coming home, you'll see!' But his parents did not seem to hear him. Then the image of them began to fade in his mind. Luke was about to open his eyes, feeling sick with disappointment, when suddenly the bright light in his head began to darken. Luke felt as if he were tumbling into a heavy, suffocating blackness. He felt ice cold and began to panic. The purple face of a Deep Eeshu reared up and stared at him with its bottomless, black eyes. Luke cried out with horror and looked around him. The Eeshu were staring at him, looking concerned. Keeya, who sat beside him, took his hand and squeezed it. The warmth of her touch spread gradually through his chilled body and he felt some of his horror begin to fade. Coryan then broke the silence.

'The Wise Ones want you to know that your parents will hear you, if you keep thinking of them and sending them your message. Also, that you will face some challenges that may seem impossible or dangerous, but I am to tell you that you will survive and achieve all that you are here to do, as long as you listen to all that we teach you.'

Luke felt disturbed by the ominous words but he quietly nodded, clinging to the fact that he would be able to bring his parents some hope, some comfort, through his thoughts.

The weary travellers retired thankfully to bed, hoping the storm would die out before they continued their journey the next morning. Alas it was not to be. When Luke broke from troubled dreams he could feel the motion of the stormy seas in the water that surrounded him, despite the shelter of the cave. Unwilling to go back to his horrible dreams of darkness and suffocation, Luke turned to see if Biblyan was awake. He was surprised to find the Eeshu boy was missing. Luke searched around the spacious cave home but realised not only was Biblyan missing from the cave but also that it was still before dawn and no one else was yet awake.

Puzzled, Luke cautiously left his host's cosy home and made his way to the entrance cavern. He was just in time to see Biblyan kicking upwards towards the surface. Out here in the open sea the water was so agitated by the storm that Luke struggled to stop himself being hurled against the rock face. He wondered if it was such a good idea, trying to follow Biblyan. On the other hand he was curious as to why the boy had left so mysteriously, and all alone.

Summoning all his strength, Luke kicked out and upwards, following the disappearing figure of his friend. Luke soon became exhausted by the force of the sea and often lost sight of his friend in these unfamiliar waters. Finally however Biblyan seemed to tire too. Luke watched the Eeshu boy pause within the calmer waters of a small natural harbour, grasping his sides, trying to regain his breath. Fortunately, Luke had plenty of bobbing boats to hide behind. He, too, tried to gain his breath back as he clung onto a heavy anchor chain. A curious lobster paused at his feet and Luke smiled faintly at the little creature. When he looked up again he felt suddenly anxious.

Biblyan had moved on and Luke couldn't see him anywhere. Where might he have gone?

Hurriedly Luke scoured the area then saw to his amazement that Biblyan was clinging to the harbour rocks, his face contorted. Luke immediately realised what was happening, for he had seen Keeya experience the same agony. Biblyan was trying to transform! But why here, and why now? Luke attempted to get as close as he could. Biblyan remained so locked in his own personal struggle that he remained oblivious of Luke. After a while, Biblyan dragged himself up the steps and out of the water. Luke followed as closely as he could. He remembered how badly things had turned out when Keeya had emerged onto land.

Luke remained there, watching the cold dawn light penetrate the stormy water. He fretted for the safety of his friend. Finally he could bear the suspense no longer and he called out in his mind to Biblyan, asking where he was, and was he safe? There was no reply.

Luke drew a deep breath and attempted a partial transformation for himself, hoping to at least remain above the surface long enough to locate his friend. He crawled cautiously up the harbour steps, just as his friend had done. When he felt certain that there were no human sounds coming from above, he attempted once more to breathe air.

The waves, which crashed against the harbour wall, tried to drag him back under but Luke clung to the slimy rock, finding a large metal ring buried in the wall which he used to haul himself higher. Luke was elated to have managed to breathe for several minutes in the air. His lungs began to protest and he knew he would have to dive back into the sea very soon. He looked urgently around at the pretty harbour, full of colourful red houses with grassed roofs. The houses were closed up, their inhabitants still asleep, and no humans were visible in the quiet streets. Just when he had given up, he spotted Biblyan. The Eeshu boy stood tall and pale, with his long, ice white hair hanging limp and flat against his broad back. He was holding the hand of a human girl who stood beside him. She had a pretty face and long, dark blonde hair. Biblyan was talking urgently to her. She appeared to be crying.

Despite feeling surprised and curious, Luke could delay no longer and he threw himself into the raging sea before he suffocated. Recovering beneath the waves, Luke agonized as to whether he should head back to the cave, or remain a while and question Biblyan when he returned to the sea. Luke decided on the latter course of action, partly because he was not entirely sure of his way back but mostly because he was longing to question his friend about the human girl. It was surely no chance meeting, for they clearly knew each other and Biblyan had taken a huge risk coming here at all. Who was the girl?

As the day lightened Luke began to worry about Biblyan's safety near humans in his vulnerable, transformed state. Luke heard a sudden crash in the water beside him and he knew that Biblyan had returned to the sea. He watched Biblyan writhe for a few moments as his lungs struggled to breathe in water. Finally he mastered himself, his long body arched in the familiar Eeshu form and he was able to join Luke, who waited patiently beside him.

Biblyan shot Luke an angry glance, which made Luke blush with guilt. Then, without speaking, Biblyan swam out into the open waters and Luke followed him. Biblyan maintained a cold silence the whole way back. He had blocked his thoughts from Luke but his emotions were so powerful their vibrations were tangible in the water around him. He ignored Luke's entreaties to explain about the girl but when they reached the cave entrance he took Luke firmly by his arm and made him swear to secrecy.

'Now you have spied out my secret, I am forced to confide in you. All you need to know is that I met Hanna when she was a little girl. I saved her from drowning. As I carried her to shore she opened her eyes and looked at me. I was so surprised to see her awake, looking directly at me and I knew she could see me. Young human children are still so pure they can see us sometimes. There was something special about the connection we had, and as I went to leave her she made me promise that I would come and see her again. I did so happily, as I have always been fascinated by land people but I had to make her swear not to tell anyone about me. That was thirteen of your human years ago and I have become very fond of her indeed.' Here he hung his head, blushing.

'How did she know to meet you today?' asked Luke curiously.

'She can hear my messages in her dreams, so she always knows when I am near. Our friendship is unique. I have never wanted any other Eeshu to hear of it. I do not think Grandfather would approve. Not that it matters now. Her family are moving to Denmark, to live in a city, and I do not think I will be able to see her again.'

'But isn't that for the best...' began Luke, but Biblyan's glare stopped his words.

'Why is it for the best? Because I am not a land creature, like you?'

'No! It's just that you live for hundreds of years, and she will get old and will die long before you. I thought perhaps it's better to let go now, rather than face losing her after years together.'

Biblyan was incensed by Luke's words.

'Do you think I am afraid of watching her age and die? It is better to enjoy my time with her now than to miss having something special, just because of the pain of future loss! Is that how you humans live? You cannot have any kind of life at all if you are so afraid of love.'

Biblyan shook his head in disgust but said no more. Instead he turned his head away for privacy, but Luke could feel the turbulent emotions emanating from his friend. Luke felt rather awkward, not really understanding the emotions but feeling sorry for his friend.

The boys stole back quietly to their dwelling where the others were up and about, preparing for their onward journey. Coryan and Keeya looked closely at the boys but made no inquiry about their absence. Luke felt that Coryan knew something but nothing was said.

They made fond farewells to Biblyan and their hosts. Luke looked anxiously at Biblyan, not wanting to leave without knowing things were alright between them. Biblyan gave him a slight smile and Luke felt reassured. Then the travellers embarked once more into icy waters.

They swam day and night, up into the Arctic seas, pausing only for a few hours to rest beneath an oil platform that was richly draped in tasty sea plants. Luke was struggling with the freezing temperatures as they travelled towards permanent night. They skirted the volcanic slopes of Iceland and by the next day, after very little sleep, they approached the coast of Greenland.

Luke had become slower and unhappier with every mile. Coryan and Keeya took turns to support him but as soon as they left him on his own he struggled to keep up. The sea creatures and plants became less varied and the water became clouded with blocks of ice floating above them. Pale, jellied creatures pulsed past, sizzling with electric colours. The Eeshu took shelter beneath an iceberg, worrying as to how to help Luke combat the cold.

Suddenly some mischievous seals appeared from nowhere, wanting to play, and for the first time in days Luke began to smile a little. Even Coryan relaxed and their weariness was momentarily forgotten as they dived and chased with the playful seals.

In a moment the mood changed. The seals barked in terror as a huge polar bear crashed into the water from the iceberg above. He was majestic but merciless. He captured a young female seal, dragging her up to the surface. Luke was horrified and clung to Keeya as he felt the screams of the victim. He felt sick to his stomach and began to shudder with cold and shock. Coryan swam up to his young charges and embraced them both, his face grim but his arms gentle.

'That is the balance of nature, that all animals must eat to live and all must die at some time. That seal lost her life but it has meant that the bear can live another day and he has a right to life too. Once death took her she did not suffer and her soul will be happy in the light again.'

Luke could not respond, the truths seemed too cruel and brought him little comfort. The cold was beginning to worry him too, what could he do to stop shivering? How could he survive the night without shelter?

Just as despair began to take hold of him, a floating piece of ice smiled at him. Luke realised with a shock that the ice was in fact one of the Arctic Eeshu, a girl, who had come to greet them. The skin of the Eeshu girl was ghostly white, with tinges of turquoise around the lips, fingers nails and ears. Her hair was transparent. But it was her eyes that transfixed Luke. Though they were the palest blue they emitted a powerful light that seared into his mind. The Arctic Eeshu girl stared fixedly at him. Taking his hands, she concentrated a wave of warmth into them. That warmth then swept through his shivering body, from his numbed scalp down to his icy toes. But best of all it warmed his heart, burning away the feelings of despair and horror.

When the Arctic Eeshu let go of his hands, he gave her a huge smile of gratitude. She greeted Coryan and Keeya then led them all downwards to her home. Beneath the ice floes was a stunning vista of homes carved from ice. The ice-homes were surrounded by gardens of kelp and sea vegetables. The whole town was lit from beneath by a green light, generated from phosphorescent plants. It created a feeling of daytime, for the seabed was so bright in contrast to the permanent darkness that existed above the surface. Luke found it strange, seeing an Eeshu town built in open sea rather than burrowed into solid rock. He was even more surprised to learn that it was newly built. Coryan explained to him,

'As the waters freeze with the onset of winter, boats cannot pass this way and so it leaves the seabed free and safe from human interference. Soon the water at the surface will seal over entirely and it is only at the sea floor that the Eeshu can freely move about.'

'Where do they live the rest of the year then?' asked Luke, hungrily accepting some food from a smiling Eeshu lady.

'They withdraw to the very heart of the Arctic seas, beneath the permafrost, where they work at healing the Earth. They are so finely attuned to their environment that when they die their bodies melt and reform as part of the ice caps.'

After being shown to their accommodation, the travellers were invited to join a special feast that was being held in honour of Keeya and her coming of age. It seemed that wherever in the world they travelled, she was known and loved. She had been given a thick, long sleeved robe which looked lovely and warm and Luke eyed it enviously. He had not been forgotten however and a long black robe was presented to him. He put it on and touched the material tentatively, for it had a texture that reminded him of leather.

'It is the skin of a seal recently killed by a polar bear. It is thick and strong and will keep you warm, as it kept the seal warm,' said one of their hosts cheerfully.

Luke looked at the garment in horror and tried to remove it, but Keeya stopped him.

'No, Luke, it will help you to survive here until we have achieved all that we came for. The seal has no use for this now, just as that fisherman you saw drown no longer needed his old body.'

Luke looked sadly down at the warm pelt that enveloped him and reluctantly admitted that it made him feel better able to deal with the cold.

After the feast there was the usual Gathering and Luke happily settled into the magic that it created both in his mind and his body. He sent his thoughts out to his parents then asked for help in learning transformation so that he could return home. When he finally went to bed he realised he was feeling more peaceful than he had done in a long while.

5

DEATH AND LIGHT

Luke was woken from his sleep by Keeya, who was shaking him urgently.

'Wake up, Luke! The magic lights are dancing tonight. You need to bathe in them, as the Wise Ones have asked you to do.'

Grumpily, Luke rubbed his tired eyes and reluctantly left his cosy bed to follow Keeya out into the chilled midnight waters. Directly above the Eeshu town a huge gap had been hewn out of the surface ice, exposing the sky above and the waves of green light that swept across the night. Laughing Eeshu were soaring upwards towards the gap, many thrusting their faces into the open air above. Green, pink and blue burst into the blackness like silent fireworks. The atmosphere amongst the Arctic Eeshu was one of happiness and excitement.

Luke felt infected by their laughter and eagerly surged upwards to the surface, looking in amazement at the light display above him. Luxuriously he lay back, enjoying the colourful sight. A small tail of soft green expanded out from the horizon, like an emerald-green genie emerging from an unseen lamp. It spread into a huge cloud of green. Then it faded and another swathe of light danced into view. Behind the folds of green Luke could see the cold, white stars glittering against the black sky. The night seemed to sigh for a moment then another thick wave of green rolled and danced across his vision. He felt himself lost in the play of light, drawn upwards into its dancing folds.

His body tingled as if it were absorbing energy from the lights. The tingling travelled from his scalp and into his brain. Then the sensation flowed down into his heart, making him shiver with a strange joy and excitement. He could feel his mind rising out of his head and he had a giddy sense of leaving his body. He looked down in a daze and saw his very own face staring back at him. It was the first time he had seen his face in its Eeshu form and he marvelled at how strange and unfamiliar he looked. His mind hovered over his supine body. He felt disembodied but not scared, just curious. He could see and feel but he felt so light that it was like flying. His conscious self floated high out of the water and into the open air, then higher and higher. All the time the sky continued its dazzling light display and now he was floating in amongst it. He looked around him and felt as if he were glimpsing another parallel world that flickered across this Earth for a few magical moments. Faces and forms appeared in the curtains of light. Luke realised he was being a granted a peep into another light-filled world.

He looked down again and saw that he had floated so high that the gaping hole in the ice, filled with eager Eeshu faces and from which he had emerged, was just a black speck in a desert of ice and snow. Still he felt no fear. The higher his conscious self rose, the more joyous he became. Am I dying? he wondered, feeling at peace with the idea.

He rose out of the colours into cool darkness, then in the darkness he saw a speck of white. The tiny speck expanded slowly into a circle of brilliant light and then he was entirely engulfed in the light. He was the light. The joy he felt was indescribable. Then a voice spoke to him, a man's voice. It was strong and clear though the voice had no face or form.

'Luke, traveller-of-light. We are offering you a choice. Come with us into the light, or return to Earth, to your friends and continue your mission.'

When Luke thought of his Eeshu friends he was filled with affection for them, but he had no hesitation in replying,

'I want to stay here, in the light.'

The male voice was silent. Instead of words, images appeared in Luke's mind. First he saw his family, anxious but full of hope that he would return to them, and he felt his heart ache for them. Then he saw himself return to his world as a young man, working with the Eeshu to help create a healthier world, combating pollution and the destruction of sea life. He saw a world on the brink of disaster slowly being restored to a world of beauty. It was a relief to see all this but Luke could not see what his part in all this was.

The voice answered his unspoken questions.

'You were chosen to help unite the world of the Eeshu and the world of humans, in order to prevent irreversible destruction of the ecosystem of your planet. You have a unique experience and understanding of both your worlds that will enable you to save your world from future catastrophe. You are never alone, for we will always help you. This is your choice, however. You can join us here in the light, or you can return to your planet and help to save it.'

Luke knew what he must do but still he could not make the decision. To leave this feeling of utter joy and belonging and return to a difficult and pain-filled world was too hard. He couldn't bear it.

But at last, thinking of his parents, of Keeya, Coryan and Biblyan, he knew he had to return. Even as he admitted this to himself, Luke felt himself slowly falling downwards. He entered the darkness, then the coloured lights in the night sky and he felt himself growing heavier and heavier.

Looking downwards he saw the speck of black in the snow growing wider. Luke saw his Eeshu body floating in the water and with a sickening feeling he crashed back into himself. He lay still, feeling sick and giddy and still a little bit disconnected to his body. Gradually his senses returned. He could hear the harmonious voices of the Eeshu around him, singing of happiness and healing their ice-filled world. He felt a wave of fondness for them all, but part of him grieved to have left that cradle of light.

When Luke woke the next morning, he began to doubt his extraordinary experience of the night before, thinking it must have been strange and vivid dreams. But he knew that something fundamental had shifted inside of him. He felt powerful, yet peaceful. When he joined Keeya and Coryan he suddenly felt a welling of tenderness for them and gave each of them a big hug. Both looked surprised, but pleased, though there was something in Coryan's eyes that was touched with a deep sadness.

Keeya said eagerly,

'Grandfather is taking us to the very North, as close to the Pole as we can travel in water. He said there is something very special there that he would like to show us.'

Yesterday Luke would have felt glum at the thought of travelling into deeper darkness and cold, but today he felt invincible. He happily set off with his two companions, looking forward to more adventures.

The sea ice was deep and in places it created almost impassable cliffs and ravines that they had to wriggle and twist through. The creatures that lived there in such an extreme environment were sparse but quite amazing in their own way. Luke saw little shrimp creatures feasting on unseen microscopic plants and occasionally a jellied animal would shoot past, emitting pulses of coloured bioluminescent lights as it passed through the dark waters.

The Eeshu travellers had to consciously boost their own light to help guide themselves in this strange, icy seascape, using laughter and happy thoughts to give themselves an extra glow. This, however, also betrayed Coryan's thoughts, for at times his glow dipped low. The sadness that emanated from him began to worry Keeya and Luke.

The frozen sea gradually became impassable. Luke felt trapped between the walls of solid ice. He looked around in fear, wondering how they could escape. Without a word Coryan suddenly dived downwards, between the narrow walls of ice. Luke and Keeya followed for what felt like ages. Luke expected to see the sea floor at any moment, but the blackness was an abyss and he began to feel he would never escape this place. Keeya must have felt anxious too, for she felt for his hand.

They continued to dive down after Coryan in silence, hoping that any moment this chilling descent would end. Just when their lungs began to feel crushed by the water above them, they saw a white light glimmering below them. The light was coming from a cave in the ice wall and they swam eagerly towards it. As they approached the cave, the light became so intense they had to shield their eyes from its glare. Finally the light was bright enough to banish all darkness around them.

As Luke's eyes adjusted to the brightness he saw this cave was not a primitive hole. It was not merely a cavern but the entrance to an underground land. It was formed from a type of white, calcified rock that was stained with streaks of pink and brown minerals. This white rock formed valleys, hillsides and beautiful stalagmite structures that soared up from the floor like pillars. The valleys were clothed in green pastures of sea grass, algae and plants. Yellow, red and pink sponges were dotted amongst them, appearing like colourful flowers. Beautiful and bizarre species of jellyfish, starfish and crabs, never seen by humans, lived and thrived in this place. The blazing light, its source as yet unclear, was like sunshine over a green and lush paradise.

Set in the rock walls of this huge cavern were familiar Eeshu cave homes and sea igloos dotted the green valleys like little farmsteads. All were deserted. The scale of this undersea paradise was so vast they could not see the end reaches of the cavern, it spread far and wide for miles about them.

As the travellers came further in, they were all drawn towards the most remarkable feature of this landscape and the source of this wondrous light. It was a glittering pyramid, about fifty metres high, made of a transparent crystal rock that mirrored back the landscape surrounding it. Though it radiated a powerful light, the light was so diffused that their proximity to the pyramid did not blind them. They swam fast towards the crystal, eager to investigate it and enjoy the warmth that it radiated. Luke examined the pyramid closely. It was as if a rainbow was contained inside, for every colour seemed to be captured inside the crystal. At the very base of the prism there was a pool of clear liquid trapped within it, like a large bubble. Luke touched the pyramid, stroking the slippery, flat sides which were free of any tool mark. A throb of energy shot up his arm and his hand flew off in shock.

'Is this a diamond?' he asked Coryan.

The old Eeshu shrugged.

'This is a single piece of crystal, perhaps a diamond, which has been here for millions of years. This pyramid is so old that no records exist of how it was made, or by whom. Very few Eeshu visit it, except the Arctic Eeshu, who live here during the summer months.'

'Grandfather, why did you bring us here? Why does it make you so sad?' Keeya asked bluntly, worry in her face as she scanned her grandfather's sad expression.

'It is not this place that makes me sad, how could it? It has a very special power, this pyramid. You see the light that it makes? Some Eeshu say this pyramid contains the very heart of this planet. They believe its light source is the very first spark of life on Earth. They also say that it can heal anything and that the Earth will always survive as long as the pyramid remains intact. Also, do you see that bubble of water that is captured inside the prism? It is said that the water inside is the oldest on this earth and that it contains the secret of the birth of our world, if we are able to access it.'

The travellers were hungry after their long, cold journey. They swam off into the landscape, eagerly sampling the plants that grew abundantly about them. After they had gorged on as much as they could, they took more to fill their bags. Then they gazed around them, delighting in everything that they saw.

Meadows of sea grass were being delicately nibbled by shoals of fishes and a herd of sea mammals, like miniature dugongs, were grazing contentedly beside them. Luke and Keeya discovered natural springs of fresh, steaming hot water that bubbled up from the floor and formed white-encrusted pools. Tentatively, they dipped their toes in the hot water and gasped at the temperature.

'Oh Luke, it reminds me of the tropical seas. The waters there are so balmy you just want to laze in it all day. I need a chill in the water to keep me awake and active,' she giggled, gazing at her reddened, webbed toes.

Luke looked around him, grinning.

'This place is awesome; it's the most incredible place I have ever seen.' He smiled at Keeya and held her hand, wanting to share the joyful feeling inside of him. Keeya blushed and looked away but allowed her hand to remain in his. They spent a while lounging by the hot springs, not speaking but content to look around them.

Luke looked at Keeya more closely, wondering how he could have ever imagined her to be ugly. She seemed lovelier to him every day. Here in this bright light he noticed how her skin had a pearlised appearance, satiny and glowing, and how fine and delicate her features were. She pretended not to be aware of his scrutiny and kicked her legs playfully in the heated water. As her dress rose up her leg, Luke noticed a jagged white scar around her knee which he had never seen before. Frowning, he asked her,

'How did you get that scar? It must have hurt, it looks quite serious.'

Abruptly, Keeya pulled her robe down.

'I don't remember,' she muttered but she could not prevent an emotion of fear and sadness emanating from her. Then with a sigh she added, 'I was a baby when I was injured. I was attacked by something, a shark perhaps, and my mother died saving me.' Keeya was quiet for a moment. Then she added, 'That is all I know, for I have never wanted to know more. I never knew my mother, though she speaks to me in dreams sometimes. I have a hair comb of hers that my father gave me. Here.'

Keeya took a delicate, coral hair comb from her bag and

handed it carefully to Luke. He politely examined it before handing it back to her. She caressed it and tenderly put it back in her bag.

Luke would have liked to remain by the hot pools but Keeya felt it was time to leave. They found Coryan still seated beside the pyramid, his eyes closed. Hearing their approach he slowly opened his eyes and smiled at them.

'Are we to stay here a while, Grandfather?' asked Keeya, happily chasing after a curious shoal of golden, transparent fish. The fish looked like pieces of coloured glass, their organs visible to the eye.

'I wish we could my child, but once we feel sufficiently rested we should return to our Arctic friends before the sea freezes so completely it becomes impassable. Besides, these dark waters are not safe at this time of year.' Coryan frowned.

'What are you afraid of, Grandfather?' asked Keeya, looking surprised at the thought of him feeling fear.

'Down in these Arctic depths there are other ancient things that should not be here.'

Coryan visibly shuddered and Luke felt a chill of terror down his own spine, though he could not imagine what the fear was of.

Coryan continued,

'It was important to show you this sacred place Keeya, for you will be the guardian of our world when I die and this must be kept safe. Mankind does not yet know of its existence but one day they may develop the technology to access all the secrets of the Eeshu world and we must be prepared to save it.'

Regretfully they left the secret cavern. The waters outside seemed even darker and colder after the warm light they had enjoyed. Their Eeshu glow seemed feeble in comparison. They maintained silence as they swam upwards, concentrating on speed to escape the depths and begin the return to their Arctic friends. There was an added feeling of fear and Luke could not wait to escape the utter darkness. Images of an ancient, hideous, monstrous face flashed into his mind and he looked nervously around him. Keeya and Coryan seemed to feel the same anxiety. A flicker of movement caught his eye. Luke gasped and turned, scanning the impenetrable darkness with fear prickling his scalp. Keeya swam close and hugged him nervously whilst Coryan paused.

'What did you see?' he asked Luke, his voice reassuringly calm.

'I...I don't know. I thought I saw something move, but I'm not sure.'

They continued onwards, with more urgency. They were now closer to the surface and their progress was made even more difficult by the lumps of ice that blocked their way. They never lost the feeling of something malevolent behind them. A horrible, unseen energy seemed to be closing in on them. Their growing fear made their progress even more stumbling.

The channels between walls of ice were at times so narrow they could scarcely get through. One channel was so tight that Coryan's huge torso became jammed. He struggled to free himself, twisting painfully against the unforgiving ice. Scarlet blood began to stain the water and Keeya sobbed with concern at the sight of her grandfather's bleeding chest. Frantically Luke and Keeya hacked at the ice with their knives but the ice was so hard they could only carve off slivers at a time.

Luke was working at the ice behind Coryan, Keeya from the other side. Suddenly Luke felt the water surge against him as if pushed forward by something powerful. All three of them felt it and looked fearfully down the channel behind them but they could see nothing. Luke felt extremely vulnerable and hacked and chiselled more frantically than before. Coryan struggled once more to free himself. Blood from his damaged shoulder floated around them.

An unearthly moan reached them. It was so deep the vibrations of it hurt their ears. They heard a crash and a shock wave of water surged over them, forcing them to cling to each other, trying to keep anchored. Keeya hastily took a handful of sea plants out of her bag, dropping some as her hands were shaking so much. She squeezed the plant's glutinous juice over her grandfather's skin, trying to ease him out of the ice trap.

With a mighty roar Coryan writhed and struggled his shoulders out of the ice as the whole ice wall began to crack and split around them. There was another ear-splitting crash and the water shuddered. Some unseen force was breaking down the ice walls, trying to reach them. They were being hunted.

Coryan grabbed his young charges as the ice channel began to collapse. They swam fearfully through falling shards of lethal ice blocks. Behind them the unseen force gave another deep moan which shuddered through them, shaking their nerves to pieces. As the ice world tumbled down around them the Eeshu dodged and weaved their way through, Coryan leaving a stream of blood behind him.

The unseen monster behind them roared with blood lust. The roar was so close that Luke had to look behind him. He screamed at the sight of the most hideous, demonic face he had ever seen. It was the face of an ancient marine dinosaur, full of jagged teeth in a reptilian face, eyes black and pitiless. The energy from it was so primitive. Luke sensed its hunger and desperation and he almost fainted with terror. The monster was clearly struggling to make its way through the collapsing ice channel but Luke knew it was powerful enough to reach them. He sobbed with despair as he and his companions raced for their lives.

'We must leave the sea and climb onto land, it is the only way we can escape it,' Coryan shouted to Luke. They soared upwards, to a gaping hole in the surface ice. Behind them Luke could see the enormous body of the monster. It had a long, thick tail that it was using to smash the ice away.

Coryan threw Keeya out of the water with a tremendous push, then grabbed Luke and did the same. There was no time for a full transformation but as soon as they hit the snow they struggled to control their minds and breathing, crawling through the snow and blizzard as far from the gap in the ice as they could. Despite his struggle against suffocation, Luke was aware that Coryan had not yet joined them. He dragged himself back to the gap in the ice, just in time to see Coryan trying to haul himself out. Luke wanted to help but he was too weak from lack of oxygen.

Coryan gave a sudden roar of pain. A look of horror twisted his face and he struggled to drag himself onto the ice. Luke grabbed at Coryan, his hands slipping on the blood that streamed from Coryan's shoulder wound, but it was hopeless. Coryan's great body spasmed and he screamed in agony. Luke knew the monster had caught hold of him. As the mighty Eeshu was dragged back downwards into the icy sea, he cried out to Luke,

'Save Keeya!'

Coryan then disappeared from sight, dragged down into the depths by the monster. Luke and Keeya continued to stare in disbelief at the gap in the ice, willing for Coryan to suddenly appear. They sat in shock, gasping for breath as they struggled to master their breathing. All they could hear was the wind screaming about their ears, and their vision was blocked by the snow that clung to their lashes. The cold was unbearable. They knew that if they did not re-enter the water they would soon die, but still they sat immobile, shocked and despairing.

Gradually the numbness took over all their senses and they felt unconsciousness creeping up on them. Wearily Luke rested his head in the snow, welcoming the empty darkness closing in on his mind. But the darkness refused to envelop him. Instead a light glowed about him. Faces appeared around him, whispering insistently.

'Luke, wake up, this is not your time. Take Keeya with you, for you both still have work to do.'

With a sigh, Luke roused himself and groped around for Keeya. She was now lying unconscious beside him. With a huge effort he pulled her towards the gap in the ice, which was rapidly re-freezing over. He had to stamp on the ice to clear it again and with a groan he plunged into the sea, dragging Keeya's limp form with him. His brain was still so numb with shock he felt no fear of meeting the monster, he felt nothing at all. But there was no sign of the beast, nor of Coryan.

'He knew. He knew this was going to happen. He knew.' Luke found himself repeating this realisation over and over like a mantra. He said it to himself for hours, holding that single thought in his mind so as to block out more painful thoughts. Using blind instinct, he made his way slowly, numbly, back to the Eeshu community, towing the motionless body of Keeya beside him.

Luke allowed the other Eeshu to take Keeya from him. Then he wordlessly stumbled to a bed, unable to speak or explain to the anxious Eeshu what had happened and why Coryan was absent. When he woke up his body felt bruised and achy and his heart was sick with sorrow. Through his misery he heard a deep, familiar voice, calling his name. Luke sat up, amazed to find Coryan sitting on his bed, smiling at him.

'Coryan, you're alive! You escaped! How did you manage it?'

Luke sat up and hugged the old Eeshu but then he slowly drew away, puzzled.

'You feel so light. And what happened to those wounds on your body?' Luke asked the old man. Coryan's skin was smooth and unmarked.

'All healed, young one. I feel reborn and I have never felt better.' Coryan's voice was still deep and comforting but there was a new note of joy in his voice.

'How did you escape? When I saw you being dragged under, I thought the monster had killed you.'

'He did,' Coryan answered simply, still smiling calmly at the bemused young boy.

'What do you mean?' asked Luke slowly, as the truth began to dawn on him.

'It was my time to leave this world and return home to my loved ones who have passed before me. But before I leave this world completely I wanted to give you a message. I will still help you with your task when I can, for it is of great importance. Just ask whenever you need me.' Coryan then frowned in his familiar way and added, 'but you must take great care of my beloved Keeya, for she is as special and vital to this planet as you are.'

'But what task are you talking of? What must I do now?' asked Luke dazedly. Was he dreaming?

'Your task at the moment is simply to travel with Keeya across the ocean to an island near Bermuda. There you will find my son Tiyan and his wife Merya, uncle and aunt of Keeya. They can teach you things that will enable you to return to your own world and family. Then you will continue your mission on land.'

Looking at Luke's worried face he then added gently,

'Just take each day as it comes, for your journey is as important as your destination. We will all guide you, every step of the way. You are never alone.'

Coryan stood up.

'Now young Luke, I want to spend a last few moments with Keeya before I continue with my own special journey.'

The old Eeshu then turned and, smiling at unseen faces, he faded away, leaving no trace of himself behind. Luke felt a huge ache in his throat of unshed tears, yet seeing the old Eeshu one more time had been of such comfort that Luke grieved less than he thought possible. Shaking his head at the incredible vision he had just experienced, he lay down once more and fell into a long and healing sleep.

When he woke up, he found Keeya seated anxiously by his bedside. As soon as she saw him stir she flung her arms around him, sobbing.

'Oh Luke, I cannot bear it, to think Grandfather has gone. What am I to do? How can I continue this journey without him?' she said in misery, clinging to Luke for comfort.

Luke hugged her then said hesitantly,

'Did he come to see you, after he, you know..?' He could not quite finish the sentence. Keeya drew slowly away from him, looking puzzled.

'Yes, at least, I thought I was dreaming and just wishing he was still with me. Why, did you see him too?'

Luke nodded.

'Yes, and he wants us to continue our journey together. He seems to think it is very important.'

Keeya got up and looked at her hands, wringing them as she struggled with her grief. Then she became still, and nodded, as if in response to an unheard question.

'Yes,' she whispered to herself then looked directly and more calmly at Luke, though her blue eyes still brimmed with sadness. 'At least I have you, Luke. I cannot face leaving, not just yet, but when I feel a bit stronger then yes, we must carry on with our journey. Until then, I want to meditate by myself and speak with the Wise Ones. I know this pain inside of me will ease and then I will be ready.'

With a sad dignity she rose and left him. Luke watched her go, aching for her grief but admiring her courage.

Later that night the Arctic Eeshu held a special Gathering to mourn Coryan and Luke felt comforted by it. He remembered the change in himself following his experience in the Northern lights, when he had been given the choice of remaining in the light or returning to Earth. Luke knew the joy that Coryan would now be experiencing himself in that loving place of light.

Luke also realised that, in her grieving state, Keeya was in great need of his support. Now he would have to be the strong one, the one to guide and support, just as she and Coryan had supported him since his drowning, all those weeks ago. He remembered how Keeya had risked her life just to get him human food. Even a few days ago he would not have been able to find the strength for this new challenge but his experiences in the Arctic had changed him forever. He and Keeya would be able to face any danger, as long as they had each other.

6
SEA ANGELS AND SHIPWRECKS

It was another week before Keeya felt able to face the long journey onwards. As they made an affectionate farewell to their Arctic hosts, both Luke and Keeya were acutely conscious of the absence of Coryan and his strong, protective presence.

They had changed their original travel plans. Although their destination lay directly across the heart of the Atlantic Ocean, they feared the vast deep and its hidden monsters. They chose instead to keep close to shorelines wherever possible and where the food would be abundant. This would mean travelling around the southern tip of Greenland and then across the sea to Canada, before travelling southwards down the American coastline to Bermuda.

Staying close to land and humans meant they had an increased chance of being caught in fishing nets, or being poisoned by polluted sea plants. Luke had come to realise just how much human activity was affecting life in the sea. It was not just the damage caused by overfishing, bringing species to near extinction, nor even all the plastic rubbish that was choking the seas. Luke had found to his cost that waste chemicals from farms and industries were leaking into the sea. He had experienced sickness from the sea plants infected with these poisons.

As they moved southwards Luke was aware of other sea creatures moving away from the encroaching Arctic ice, escaping the sea before the surface froze over completely. Newly-born icebergs were filling the ocean, making convenient islands to shelter beneath. Luke and Keeya found their mournful thoughts distracted by the company of excited whales, dolphins and shoals of fish that were migrating to warmer waters.

For the most part, Luke and Keeya's journey was quiet and introspective. Luke could not stop thinking about the horror of Coryan's death. He thought about the world of the Eeshu, the human world and wondered how he fitted in. What could he possibly do to bridge these two worlds? Meanwhile, Keeya's thoughts were wholly of her beloved grandfather and how she would face her life without his loving guidance. Yet for all that, when they paused for food and rest, there was a comfortable companionship between them.

Luke was enjoying the changing seascapes. He had never imagined crossing to the other side of the world and he was excited by these new vistas. After a day or so of hugging shorelines they reached a point where the seabed sloped down steeply to dark, deeper waters. Keeya recognised this as the start of their crossing over the sea to the Canadian coast but she had not yet told Luke of the vast sea canyon that they must first cross.

'Luke, we have a long crossing to make without much food available, let us fill our bags with enough plants to last us a day or so. Also, there are no caves or shelter in this part of the deep so we cannot pause to rest for long. Are you strong enough to make it that far?'

Luke shrugged.

'I don't know, but if you can do it, so can I.'

Keeya nodded but hesitated still. Luke knew that she was thinking of the monster beneath the ice cap and he felt apprehensive too. But there was nothing to be gained, lingering here, unless they wanted to become food for polar bears.

'Come on Keeya, let's keep close together. You know, Coryan told me that he would be with us for this journey and that we are never alone. Let's think of him swimming alongside us, taking care of us.'

Luke held out his webbed hand. Keeya grasped it, her lips trembling with emotion. Then with a shared smile they launched forward, watching the seabed fall away beneath them as they headed into the deepening sea. Soon they lost sight of the seabed altogether and Luke felt nervous and vulnerable, swimming over the unseen and unknown.

They had been swimming over the abyss for a few hours, when a large fishing trawler thundered dangerously close by. It was hunting the abundant shoals of fish. Keeya and Luke dived down as steeply as they could to avoid it. Luke cringed as he heard the screams of creatures caught in the undiscriminating nets. The deeper waters became heavy on his chest and he began to feel faint.

'Luke, breathe slowly and deeply and imagine your lungs full of oxygen. If you relax, you can allow your body to adjust to these deeper waters', Keeya advised him soothingly.

Luke followed her advice and found that he was able to master his breathing well enough to cope with the change in water pressure, although the weight of the water still made his head ache. It was so dark in these waters that it was not clear when day became night. Luke knew he was beginning to tire so he indicated to Keeya that he needed food and rest. He was intrigued when Keeya removed something from her waist bag and unravelled a ball of twine. At the end of the twine was a large, flaccid balloon, made from a stretchy type of sea plant. Keeya blew into the balloon and it swelled into a large buoy which she then released above them. She wrapped the twine about their wrists so that they could remain safely together without being pulled apart by the strong current that was beginning to tug at them.

They nibbled at the supplies they had brought along but there was a strange atmosphere around them and both felt nervous and unsettled. They decided after only a brief rest to move on again but then a deep groan quivered in the water about them and they froze with fear. Again came the moan and Luke began pulling at the anchoring twine that was wrapped about his wrist. He struggled to escape, wanting to get away from this place as quickly as possible. As soon as they were both released Keeya broke away but instead of swimming onward she unexpectedly dived downwards into the abyss.

'Keeya, no! We have to get away from here, can't you hear the monster?' Luke called anxiously after her retreating feet, but she continued downwards. After a moment of indecision, Luke gave a fretful cry then dived down after her.

'Keeya, what are you doing? We are in danger and we need to get out of here as quickly as possible!'

'No, Luke, come and see. It is not a monster. Come,' replied Keeya calmly.

Still anxious, Luke caught up with her. Beneath them they could barely see the sea floor. As Luke squinted into the gloom, he began to make out a faint glow. It outlined a large shape. Was it a shipwreck? The large shape gave another long, mournful sound and he knew it was some huge sea monster.

'Oh Luke, it is a sea angel! And I recognise his song, it is dear old Grandfather.'

'Sea angel? Grandfather?' questioned Luke, alarmed at the huge size of this groaning monster but reassured by Keeya's evident pleasure at seeing the creature.

They finally reached the huge body that lay on the seabed. Luke recognised it at once. It was a whale. With its distinctive large head, mottled, dark skin and vast size he realised it must be one of the legendary blue whales. The creature was the size of a small cruise ship and it was hard not to feel intimidated and overawed but Keeya boldly went up to it. She lovingly caressed its great nose and sang soothingly to it.

'Why do you call it a sea angel?' asked Luke, cautiously reaching a hand to touch the immense, barnacle-encrusted beast.

'Because they have a soul as pure and wise as an angel. And this dear old man has been swimming the oceans as long as I have. I call him "Grandfather" because he has had many children and grandchildren and he is old for a sea angel.'

'Why is he down here? What's wrong with him?'

'He is here to die. It is his time to go and he is calling to his children to say goodbye,' she answered. The thought of her own grandfather's death made her sigh deeply with sadness.

As if in answer, the dying whale gave another long, mournful sigh and the sound tugged at Luke's heart. Then he heard answering cries, echoing his own sadness. Above him Luke could see more blue whales arriving. They began circling above their dying patriarch. They were singing a song that was filled with emotion. Luke was moved beyond bearing. He looked at Keeya and she began to sing with them, singing of her own grandfather with love and grief. Luke swam over to her and joined in with his own voice, unable to contain the sadness inside himself any longer. He felt united with both Keeya and the whales as they expressed vibrations of love and sorrow.

Other Eeshu voices joined in but these voices were strange, so deep and resonant they made Luke's body shake. Emerging through the darkness came the Deep Eeshu, solemn, majestic and terrible, with their giant purple bodies, black eyes and long black hair that streamed out into the current. One of the Deep Eeshu came up to the eye of the dying whale, and began chanting softly to the beast. The whale gave a soft groan and the glow of light encircling the whale's body began to intensify. The singing of the whales that circled around them ceased and all present watched as the soul of the old whale gently drifted away from its aged, scarred body. There was a universal sigh, then a dark moment of sadness and loss. A few at a time, the other whales drifted past the corpse to give a farewell nudge and caress. Then one by one the sea angels moved off into the darkness, once more pursuing their solitary journeys.

Luke and Keeya remained by the dead body, overcome with emotion as they remembered Coryan. The Deep Eeshu encircled them, silent and fearsome. They were significantly larger than other Eeshu and Luke felt dwarfed by them. Keeya on the other hand seemed pleased to see them.

The leader addressed her.

'Child, it is a joy to see you amongst us, though we are deeply saddened to hear of your loss. Coryan will be much missed, and our world is more fragile without his protection. Will you travel with us, under our care? Can we give you any assistance?'

With a small shake of her head and a friendly smile she replied,

'Dear friends, it is so good to see you all, but Luke and I need to make our journey alone. Perhaps we will meet again soon, when our task is accomplished.' She then made polite farewells and the Deep Eeshu silently disappeared back into the darkness.

Luke was relieved by her refusal of their gloomy company but Keeya heard his thoughts and looked disapprovingly at him.

'You are wrong to distrust them, the Deep Eeshu are wonderful and incredibly knowledgeable. Not only are they the guardians of the creatures that live in the depths of our oceans, they are also the guardians of all Eeshu knowledge and culture. However, I know that Grandfather felt it was important that we attempt this journey on our own and that is the only reason I refused their kind offer of assistance.'

She then kicked off from the seabed, with Luke sheepishly following behind. They rose higher, where daylight still penetrated the water. Luke looked down and noticed large white structures that were set into the seabed. They looked like the fallen pillars of temples and buildings.

'Is that an old city, lying at the bottom?', he asked Keeya, keen to explore.

She shook her head.

'Those are the bones of whales that have died here. This is their final resting place, their graveyard.

Luke was surprised.

'So all the whales come to this one place to die?'

'Only the sea angels from this family. There are many other such places across the ocean floor. Sea angels have followed the same routes for thousands of years, even though over the centuries land has become sea and sea has become land. The sea angels know and remember all of this, for they pass on all their knowledge to the next generation. We Eeshu say that the sea angels are the living memory of the history of our planet's oceans. Grandfather once told me that there are creatures on land who are like this, he called them elephants. Do you know of them?'

Luke nodded, surprised at the comparison and at Coryan's knowledge. But then if you live for eight centuries you are bound to learn a few things, he thought to himself.

Their journey across the inky darkness was made difficult by the strong, icy currents that they had to fight across. Luke felt tired by the continual struggle to force his way through and he felt disorientated by the featureless darkness around them.

'How do you know your way, Keeya? Have you been this way many times before?' he asked, curious and a bit concerned that she might be lost.

'I have been this way before, when I was a small child, but you can never be lost in the ocean. The currents are like road ways which cross and divide the seas. Just by allowing yourself to feel the pull of their energy helps you to find your way. Each current carries smells and tastes from where it has been, so even in complete darkness you can have a good idea of where you are, and how far from land you are.'

Luke closed his eyes and allowed himself to be tugged at by the current. It was strongest on his left side and had a smell and taste of the polar ice. He was so absorbed trying to read the current that he began to drift into it and felt himself suddenly being swept away towards the heart of its powerful, icy energy. He opened his eyes in alarm and called out to Keeya, who swiftly dived into the pathway of the current and struggled to pull him to the edge of the current's wake. Keeya did not appear too alarmed by the incident. Instead she shook her head and laughed.

'Oh Luke, if you had stayed in that current it would have whisked you all the way back to Greenland again, and I would have had to wait an age for you to shoot on by again.'

Luke felt peeved at her laughter. He tried so hard to learn

the Eeshu ways, just as he had been told to do by the Wise Ones and it annoyed him to have his attempts mocked by Keeya. As always though, Keeya immediately understood him and explained to him in an apologetic tone,

'You see, that current is part of a gyre, a giant whirlpool that covers this area of the Atlantic. It is stirred by the cold waters of the North Pole and by the winds from the air above. This makes the currents form a continuous circle. I always imagine it as if a giant is stirring the ocean with a huge spoon, causing all us sea creatures to whizz helplessly around in a huge whirlpool. It just seemed funny to imagine you shooting round to the North Pole and back again, but I did not mean to mock you. I am so pleased that you have immersed yourself in the Eeshu way. Your knowledge and capability for one so young and inexperienced is nothing less than miraculous. Grandfather was right when he called you special.'

Luke fell silent, surprised by the compliment. He followed after Keeya with a huge smile on his face.

They had to travel across the deep for a day longer than they had planned. The powerful currents had exhausted them and slowed their progress. They preferred to take only short rests as they still found the depths a little threatening, so that when they finally reached the continental shelf of Canada they were too tired to carry on. Instead they found a small community of Eeshu who gave them shelter and rest. After another day had passed, Luke and Keeya prepared to leave. They were about to set off when the leader of their Eeshu hosts approached them with a strange request.

'On your journey southwards, please will you visit a shipwreck that you will find about a day's journey from here? We believe that you, Luke, have the ability to put some souls to rest.'

'What shipwreck is this? How will I know if I have the right one? We pass so many wrecks.' Luke was puzzled by the request. The Eeshu male explained to him,

'Oh, you will know this wreck, for it has energy such as we have never before experienced from human shipwrecks. You will feel it calling to you as soon as you are nearby. Do not be afraid, though. The Wise Ones tell us you will be able to help in a way that we cannot.'

Luke looked at Keeya, who was nodding thoughtfully.

'I know where they mean, and it is part of our journey so we will go there straight away. Now that we have crossed the deepest part of our journey I am impatient to reach my aunt and uncle. If you feel ready, shall we go?'

It was nightfall when they approached the wreck. Although the seabed seemed quiet, there was an atmosphere of sadness that lingered there. Luke was aware of a rusty taste of iron in the water which seemed to come from only a few miles away. They were travelling over a long ravine, where the continental shelf sloped steeply downwards into deeper waters. Although there seemed little of interest beneath them, Keeya spotted something and pulled Luke downwards to the sea floor. She knelt down in the sand and grasped a small object, then held it out to him. It was a decayed leather shoe. Luke looked at Keeya, puzzled, and she explained,

'Here, take this and see if you can read its energy. See what information it gives you.' She thrust the shoe into his hands as if glad to be rid of it.

Luke held the shoe for a moment, marvelling at how strange it was, to see such a familiar human object so far from the human world. He had found that shipwrecks, and even plane wrecks were sometimes interesting to investigate, but rarely haunting. Any anguish and terror experienced by the humans that perished in the wrecks did not seem to linger there. Yet he found holding a personal object such as this humble leather shoe to be very disturbing. As he ran curious fingers over the relic, he had a strong image of a small, timid lady, dressed in the uniform of a servant from long ago. She was about middle aged and was cowering with fear, sobbing and praying for help. The image was so vivid that he dropped the shoe in distaste.

Keeya continued to lead them onwards. She pointed out various scattered human items, spoons, old-fashioned wire spectacles and a collapsed leather trunk. There were also large, mangled metal parts scattered around the sea floor, parts of machinery from a ship. Luke knew that they must be close to the wreck now.

As the dark mass of the wreck came into view, the scale of it took Luke's breath away. Before them rose a colossal ship, a mass of twisted and crumpled metal lying drunkenly on a slope with its nose buried deep in mud.

Luke and Keeya cautiously approached it, drawn towards it by a horrid fascination. They swam alongside the lower portholes, peering into nothing but cold darkness. A strong atmosphere of fear brooded over the ship. Luke thought he could hear faint cries for help. Images of people scrambling to escape their imminent drowning flashed across his mind. It was so intense, so terrible, that Luke deliberately blocked any more images coming into his thoughts. He took hold of Keeya's hand, grateful for her company, and they rose higher, trying not to touch the rusty folds of decay that clothed the rotting ship. Long fringes of algae draped the railings and promenades, the funnels and gaping windows. There was nothing to see but something else was lurking there, something unseen.

Luke and Keeya remained silent, unwilling to waken any slumbering ghosts. They quietly came to rest on the upper deck, near to the centre of the broken ship. Here it had almost been torn apart and they could clearly see the different levels of decks within its interior. Despite the surrounding darkness, the ship glowed with an eerie green light. It appeared to be deserted but they had the uncomfortable feeling of being watched.

An electric feeling of horror sizzled their nerves and they held hands for comfort. Luke peered through a murky window. Ghostly faces stared sadly back at him. He drew back in shock but Keeya squeezed his arm and murmured,

'Poor souls, they need our help. Come on, let us see if we can find a way to get inside.'

Reluctantly, Luke followed Keeya. They swam down a twisted staircase that led into a weed-draped corridor, the floor thick with silt and debris. They found an engine room still filled with impressive machinery. The sense of human death seemed to linger most strongly here, down in the bowels of the boat. Humble human artefacts littered the sunken cabins. There were articles of clothing, dolls, umbrellas, shoes and books, each item soaked with fear and hysteria. It was at once both fascinating and horrifying. Luke expected to see more ghosts at every turn. They heard faint voices and cries but no more faces appeared.

Luke and Keeya now explored the upper decks, peering into the grander living quarters. In some cabins there were still human treasures to be seen, clocks, furniture and ornaments. It was like seeing a moment in time preserved forever. A diamond necklace carelessly thrown on a dressing table after a night of dancing, a sodden diary still open where its author had thrown down a pen in surprise. These human fragments appeared all so fine, so lovely and so useless.

All the time, Luke and Keeya were aware of unseen ghostly figures following them. The tension in the atmosphere was becoming unbearable. They entered an enormous room. Despite the silt and decay, Luke could see that this had once been a magnificent and luxurious place. Now it was icy cold in here, as cold as the polar waters had been. Luke could not stop shuddering.

Luke and Keeya felt reluctant to investigate any further so they remained in the centre of the room, watching nervously as the huge space slowly filled with human figures. Some were transparent, their light flickering on and off like a weak candle flame. Other figures burned strongly and angrily, their forms almost solid. Luke could see bearded men in old fashioned evening clothes, sailors, servants, humbly-dressed third class passengers and haughty ladies in fur coats and glittering jewels. The pale, flickering forms belonged mostly to children. They clung to the more solid adult forms for comfort and strength. These adult forms were the most hostile. They slowly encircled the shivering Eeshu. Luke wanted to flee this ghoulish place but Keeya held him still.

'Remember, they need you. They need your help.' Despite

her brave words Luke could feel Keeya shaking.

Luke silently asked for help. He felt his body being filled with a warm, liquid, golden light that brought warmth to his heart, giving him courage. He looked at the antagonistic ghosts pressing around him, and through their anger he began to sense their fear and despair. How can I help them? he wondered. Why do they remain here?

'Memories. Human memories keep them here', whispered familiar voices in his mind.

Luke began to understand that the golden light that filled his body was protecting himself and Keeya, like a shield against the dark energy that threatened them. Now he knew what he had to do. Summoning all the light inside of him, he imagined blasting it out in a powerful jet of compassion towards the ghosts. Looking downwards he saw a solid stream of liquid gold gushing out of his chest. The molten light swirled around the room, chasing the frightened figures of the flickering child-ghosts and curling about them in a loving embrace. The little ghosts swooned into the golden light with resigned sighs and disappeared from sight.

The adult phantoms roared with fury. They tried to strangle Luke with the dark energy that issued from them like black ink, an ink that twined itself about his throat and face. But the golden light that poured from his soul fought with their darkness. His light began to melt their darkness away. The golden light was too bright and all encompassing. The remaining ghosts had no strength left to fight it. Some of the angry ghosts sobbed in defeat, whilst others surrendered peacefully but one by one they were all swallowed up by the light.

It was as if a nuclear explosion had gone off, decimating all but Luke and Keeya. Then, as if someone had switched off the light, the golden energy that poured into Luke and out of him stopped abruptly. Luke dropped to his knees, exhausted. Keeya was gazing at him in wonder.

'Luke, that was astonishing. I have never seen anyone so powerful before.'

Too weak yet to stand, Luke shook his head.

'No Keeya, I wasn't the source of that power, it was as if someone was just using me as a channel to transmit through. I'm exhausted. Can you help me to stand up?'

Keeya scooped him up in her strong arms and swam back with him to the upper deck. When Luke had recovered sufficiently they swam thankfully away from the dead ship, moving as far away as possible from it.

They had to travel quite far into shallow, coastal waters to find shelter. After a substantial breakfast they then curled up side by side to sleep. Despite his exhaustion, Luke struggled to fall asleep. He still felt overwhelmed by the power of that golden light that had poured through him and he felt puzzled by the ghosts in the shipwreck. What had kept them bound to their grave for so long?

'Keeya, what do you know of that shipwreck? What makes it so different to other wrecks and why were the ghosts so angry with us?'

Keeya considered his question carefully before replying.

'The wreck occurred before I was born, but Grandfather remembers it. He said it was the biggest ship that had ever been built by humans and it carried so many souls on board that when it sank, the scale of the tragedy was so enormous that even the Eeshu could not save all the souls that needed us.'

Luke frowned in thought. He knew which ship it was.

'Was the ship called "The Titanic"?'

Keeya shrugged.

'Perhaps. I'm not sure. But that wreck has haunted Eeshu and human memory for so long that it seems to have preserved the horror forever. I think that is why those souls were still trapped inside the ship, for it seems humans are fascinated by the ship's story. Humans have visited the wreck several times and seem puzzled by it. We Eeshu have witnessed many human tragedies but there is something about this ship that humans cannot leave alone.'

'So why were those ghosts still trapped on the boat? Why didn't the Eeshu help their souls to the light, as they do for all the creatures that die in the sea?'

'We tried, but the power of human thought is more powerful than we Eeshu can combat. We tried over the years to help the souls move on and many have found peace but still the human obsession with this wreck had tied some of the more stubborn spirits to their grave. Now, however, you have done the impossible and released them from their endless torment.'

'Why me? Why couldn't they have used someone like you, or Coryan?'

'I truly don't know Luke, but it must be something to do with your humanity. Perhaps all of human kind have a linked consciousness that helped you connect with those ghosts in a way that an Eeshu could not have done.'

They fell silent, lost in their own thoughts, then Luke spoke quietly,

'Keeya, I think I'm beginning to understand why I'm here, and the kind of task I've been sent to do. I thought it all sounded so impossible but Coryan was right, I'm not alone, I will always have help.' He paused and then whispered as if to himself, 'But why me?'

He received no answer, either from Keeya or from the Wise Ones, and soon fell fast asleep.

7

THE SARGASSO SEA

It was a relief to leave icy seas and head southwards into warmer water. This time, instead of hugging the shorelines, Keeya led them directly across the depths towards the islands of Bermuda. She explained that it was the quickest way and that she was keen to see her aunt and uncle. Luke was happy to go along with this. He was feeling optimistic now and the golden light that had filled him in the shipwreck still lingered enough to give him the courage to face any lurking sea monsters.

As the water temperature warmed, so did their spirits. Keeya began to smile more and Luke felt excited by the new varieties of sea creatures and plants that he was discovering. They came across a hump back whale and her calf migrating southwards and they swam behind in her wake. At first the mother whale seemed concerned at their being so close to her calf but Keeya beamed reassuring thoughts to her and the whale then clicked and chattered to them, seemingly to enjoy the unexpected company. Very soon they heard more hump back whales, the song of the males vibrating thrillingly through the water. Luke had never heard this before and he marvelled at the complexity and length of their songs. He thought how great it would be, to transform into a whale, to see what it felt like to be one.

Keeya must have been thinking along these lines too, for next thing he knew a dolphin was leaping in the water beside him. This dolphin wore a long white robe and he laughed at the sight of Keeya in dolphin form. It was wonderful to see her so happy, after her week of mourning, but Luke regretted not seeing her perform the transformation. He watched her make great jumps out of the water before diving down into the blue depths. The rhythm of her movements echoed her emotions and Luke longed to join her in dolphin form. He tried surging upwards, breaking through the surface of the water, but only his head rose above the waves. His body did not seem to have the strength to propel itself upwards any higher. Sadly, he resigned himself to being in Eeshu form, envious of Keeya and more determined than ever to practice his skills in transformation.

Luke and Keeya parted company with their whale companions when they reached the circular wall of currents that create the Sargasso Sea. It was like nothing Luke had experienced so far, for this was a sea within an ocean. It was bordered not by land but by a wall of currents. There was no land except for the islets of Bermuda, which peeped above the waves somewhere near its centre.

Keeya transformed back into her Eeshu form and helped Luke break through the perimeter currents. The sea within seemed calm and sleepy. Most extraordinary of all were the huge drifts of yellowy-brown weeds which carpeted wide areas on the surface of the sea. The weed itself was bulbous with air bladders and was rather chewy but refreshing to eat. They had to be careful as they snacked on it, for other small creatures were sheltering amongst the weedy mats. Less pleasant was the plastic rubbish which also floated in drifting heaps on the water. Keeya shrugged resignedly when Luke expressed his distaste. Instead she sifted amongst the pieces of plastic bags, bottles, even flip flops, searching for anything that might be useful to them.

Keeya suggested that they rest beneath one of the drifting weed carpets, using it to protect themselves from the sun's rays.

Luke had been revelling in the warmth and brilliant light of this tropical sea but now he was beginning to feel a little bit giddy from the unaccustomed heat. Anchoring himself to Keeya with the portable buoy that Keeya kept in her bag he relaxed back, watching the dappled rays of light that pierced through the weed mat into the turquoise waters around him. His eyelids felt heavy and he closed them, welcoming the cool darkness.

Luke was surprised into wakefulness sometime later by something colliding with his legs. As he struggled to focus his sleep-blurred eyes, he realised that a young turtle had nudged him awake, clearly curious about him. He smiled and disentangled himself from the twine that bound him safely to Keeya. She was still asleep and he decided to let her rest whilst he followed the inquisitive turtle. The waters were calm and there was no strong current to pull her away. Luke swam alongside the turtle, laughing at the animal's serene and wrinkled face. It ignored him as it searched for food. The turtle seemed unconcerned that Luke was following it. Luke ran his hand over its shell, admiring the contours. The turtle became annoyed and tried to whisk away but its disgruntled expression made Luke laugh even more.

Luke turned round to check that Keeya was still nearby. She was curled about the buoy like a baby, asleep and peaceful. Her long white hair floated about her and Luke smiled to see a small seahorse had anchored its tail around the white strands.

Luke now felt wide awake again and keen to explore. Seeing movement on the sea floor he dived down to follow it, finding some eels that flicked away from him. He was then distracted by a silvery shoal of fish that shimmered around him, nibbling his hair in curiosity. He smiled and reached out to touch them but they swelled and swooped in a cloud of silver and dashed away from him in a moment.

'Hello stranger, welcome to our sea.'

The unknown voice in his head shocked Luke into stillness. He looked around him, puzzled. Gliding gracefully upwards from the turquoise depths appeared a young Eeshu girl, her hair as yellow as the seaweed above them and her eyes as turquoise as the water around them. She was quickly followed by other young Eeshu and they crowded about him, eager to meet the stranger.

The first girl spoke.

'My name is Oreeya, and these are my brothers and sisters. We are guardians of the Sargasso Sea. Who are you?'

'My name is Luke. I'm here with my friend Keeya. We're here to visit her family.'

At his words there was a ripple of excitement amongst the greeting party. 'The Chosen One. He must be the light traveller. See how strange he looks!'

Luke could hear them whispering amongst themselves. He frowned, uncomfortable with the way they were describing him.

Oreeya offered him her hand.

'Come with us, Luke. Let us show you our home.'

Luke hesitated, thinking about Keeya, who was still asleep. He looked behind him and realised he had swum away out of sight. Should he go and get Keeya, or let her rest? Despite her pleasure at swimming with the hump backs she had been looking pale with grief of late and she needed to rest. Reluctantly taking Oreeya's hand he said,

'I must be quick. I don't want to leave my friend for too long.'

'Do not worry, we will find her and bring her too. Come!'

He was dragged enthusiastically down to some coral beds, rich with life. Luke was puzzled to see a marble statue emerging from the coral shelf. He touched the marble, feeling the chiselled features of a face.

'Where does this come from? Did it fall from a wreck?' he asked his companions.

One of his new Eeshu friends smiled and shook his head.

'No, this coral has grown over an old temple that has been here for millennia. Sometimes you can see parts of the columns or statues, but we can show you better examples, come this way,' said the young Eeshu boy, keen to show Luke his home.

Luke willingly followed, full of curiosity. They came to a small underwater town that was built of marble. It was as if the sea had swallowed it from Ancient Greece, intact and perfect.

There were beautiful buildings, gardens and statues, all bustling with Eeshu. At the centre of this town was a pyramid-shaped building and the streets radiated from it like sun rays.

'Wow, I didn't know the Greeks came here!' Luke said as he swam enthusiastically towards the town, keen to explore.

'This town was not built by the people of ancient Greece. It is far older than that. This was built by our ancestors, who travelled from their native land of Atlantis in search of new lands and wealth. This town was built on a small volcanic island that sank into the sea here and we have reconstructed it to make our own homes here,' explained Oreeya.

The inhabitants of this remarkable town nodded politely as Luke approached and offered to show him into their homes. He marvelled at the scale of the place.

'How come humans haven't found out about this town? It's so large; they must have seen it through satellite pictures, or something.'

The Sargasso Eeshu frowned, confused by his reference to a satellite. Reading the images in Luke's mind, Oreeya nodded in understanding. She explained,

'Our vibration is too quick and strong for any human to see either ourselves or the objects we use, as they take on our vibration too. Unfortunately, that does not mean that we are safe from humans. They can still destroy or damage ourselves and our homes, albeit unintentionally. Chemicals spilling from the ships poison our food, and large ships and trawler nets damage our corals and destroy species of sea creatures. If humans understood as much as we do, they would realise our oceans can easily support them as well as all the creatures that live here. But they damage so much, take so much, and use so little.'

Luke listened, nodding sympathetically. His life in the ocean had already revealed these sad facts to him and he was overwhelmed by the need to stop humans behaving so thoughtlessly. But would adults listen to him? What could he do, even if he were able to return home?

Oreeya continued,

'That is why you are so important to us. You can join Eeshu and humans together and help us to help humans with our knowledge and ideas.'

'How can I help, when I can't get back to my human form?' asked Luke angrily. He felt more frustrated than ever at not being able to transform fully.

Oreeya smiled.

'You will be able to return to human form because you chose to stay and help us, and the Wise Ones will do all they can to help you achieve transformation when the time is right.'

Luke was surprised by her words. He thought to himself, 'how do they know that I chose to stay and help them? Is it possible that these Eeshu know of my journey into the light, that secret moment when I left my body and was given a choice to stay in the light or return to life on Earth? '

Then gentle voices in his head answered,

'All Eeshu knew the moment you made your choice, because that choice you made was like a drop that fell into their ocean and that drop of hope rippled out to affect every living creature in every ocean on your planet. You see, the single action of one small boy can affect a whole planet. You can make a difference. And you are never alone; we are always here to help.'

Luke felt stunned. He looked at the smiling Eeshu faces around him, felt their hope, their happiness and their faith in him. He felt faint at the responsibility on his shoulders.

'Why me?' he wondered to himself.

'Why not?' echoed back the gentle voices.

Then another realisation struck Luke. Achieving transformation was no longer a hope, it was guaranteed. It must be, if the Wise Ones had decided that he was going to save the planet. He felt a surge of elation at the idea. He was eager to share these wonderful revelations with Keeya. It was then that he remembered she was not with him, that his new friends must have forgotten to find her and bring her here. He began to feel worried and hoped she was still safely sleeping. If he left now he might reach her before she woke up.

'Luke, where are you? Luke!'

Keeya's anxious voice echoed urgently in his head and he guiltily answered back,

'I'm OK Keeya, some Eeshu friends have been showing me their home. I'll come and bring you to them.'

She made no reply but he could feel her emotions of hurt and anger vibrating through his heart and from the shades of red that filled his head. Making a quick apology to his hosts he swam off in search of Keeya.

He found her quietly sitting on the seabed, absently caressing the neck of a turtle that seemed content to rest beside her. Keeya always managed to earn the trust of the creatures around her. As Luke approached, the turtle gave him a suspicious glance and swam away. Luke sat beside Keeya, feeling guilty for worrying her and concerned by the sadness and grief that lingered in her face. Instead of reproaching him though, she said simply,

'I have spoken with my aunt, she knows we are here and will guide me to her.'

'Keeya I am so sorry, the Sargasso Eeshu said they would find you and bring you to me, but they must've forgotten...' His apology trailed off, for he had forgotten too, so absorbed had he been by the remarkable town. He awkwardly gave her a quick hug, feeling all the worse for her lack of reproach.

They continued their journey across this strange sea. Keeya was feeling her way by the thought guidance of her aunt so remained silent. Luke wanted to share with Keeya his new understanding of his role as some kind of Eeshu spokesperson to humans. Most importantly, he wanted to tell her about the certainty of his achieving transformation. But he struggled to speak to her, blocked by the negative feelings that had crept into their relationship. He wasn't sure if he should apologise again but it was Keeya who broke the silence. She said quietly,

'I was so worried when I woke to find you missing, what if you had been taken from me by some monster, just as Grandfather had been taken? I couldn't bear to think of it.'

Luke felt even worse. He explained,

'I woke up and followed a turtle for a bit, then suddenly

these Eeshu appeared. I was going to wake you, but you've been looking so tired, so unhappy recently. I couldn't bear to disturb you. But I really wanted you to be there with me. They showed me an amazing town; I've never seen one quite like it before.'

Keeya made no response, so he added,

'Just before you woke and called to me, I learnt something really exciting, and I wanted to share it with you. Apparently not only do all Eeshu seem to know who I am and why I'm here, I also learnt that I will definitely be able to learn transformation. I have to, in order to be the person I need to be, to fulfil my destiny.'

Keeya nodded thoughtfully and Luke felt a small relaxation in the tension between them. Then his thoughts returned to transformation and what returning to human form would mean to him. He thought to himself, 'I can return to Mum and Dad in human form, and at the same time I know that I can become Eeshu and still see Keeya , Biblyan and all my Eeshu friends. I could even become a dolphin and travel across the ocean whenever I want. Wow, this is going to be so amazing!' Luke felt thrilled at these thoughts. 'How wonderful, to be part of both worlds.'

Luke was as impatient now to reach their destination as Keeya. He was keen to meet the Eeshu prophets who would teach him all he needed to know. Suddenly his task no longer seemed overwhelming. It was exciting and full of wonderful possibilities.

Keeya led him to a shallow coral shelf that surrounded a tiny island on the far outskirts of the Bermuda islands. It was beautiful and the late afternoon sun was so warm and pleasant that Luke sighed blissfully. 'What a lovely place', he thought happily.

Tiyan and Merya magically appeared in front of them, as if they had been formed out of the water around them. Luke was shocked out of his happy musings.

'Keeya my love, we are so glad to see you!' Merya gave her niece a big hug, whilst Tiyan, as large and impressive as Coryan had been, nodded kindly to Keeya, squeezing her arm affectionately. Both Tiyan and Merya had the white hair and dark blue eyes of northern Eeshu but their pink skin echoed the warm hues of the coral reef. They then turned their attention to Luke, smiling at him but looking so deeply into his heart and mind that he trembled under their scrutiny, fearing they could see some of his less worthy thoughts and actions.

They seemed happy with their assessment of him for Tiyan ushered Luke towards a cave beneath the coral shelf. It was a simple, humble space, filled with plain furniture and a few decorations but it had a peaceful and comforting atmosphere that made it a pleasure to remain there. As the home was in the shallows, the high afternoon sun was able to reach its warm, bright fingers through the gaps in the coral roof above. Luke happily raised his face to the sunlight, the human side of him revelling in its warmth.

As evening approached the four Eeshu sat in a circle and entered into meditation. There was a special, serene atmosphere in the cave. They all swiftly connected with the Wise Ones, seeking their spiritual guidance. The connection felt so strong that Luke felt almost lifted out of his body, his heart and soul soaring upwards to meet the wise faces that smiled at him. He relished the blissful feelings that poured into his soul. He felt healed and strengthened. Images of his parents and his earthly life flashed before him, stirring feelings of nostalgia. It made him realise how little time he now spent thinking of his human life and family. He understood now that if he wanted to transform he would need to think like a human being again and remember what it was to be human.

After the meditation came to a gentle conclusion Tiyan turned to Luke and said,

'Luke, our friends tell me that you will be staying with us for the winter and that when the spring arrives and the whales begin their migration northwards you must follow them. Until then, you will be like a son to us and we will teach you skills that even Keeya does not yet possess.'

Tiyan then turned to Keeya,

'And you my dearest child, you will also have a unique

knowledge revealed to you, for you are as important to our planet's future as Luke is. We have been told that your souls are linked and so therefore are your destinies.'

Luke and Keeya exchanged glances and blushed.

'And now it is time for us all to rest, for we have much to teach you in a short time. Sleep well, children.'

Tiyan and Merya led Luke and Keeya to their beds, said an affectionate good night and left, leaving the young Eeshu to look at each other with shy gazes.

'Wow, it's a bit overwhelming, being responsible for the future of our planet, isn't it?' Luke said and Keeya giggled and nodded.

'You are my soul brother. I knew I found you for a reason, I knew you were important to me the moment you woke from drowning and looked at me with your grass-coloured eyes.'

They smiled shyly at each other. The knowledge of their linked destinies was not a surprise but a truth that he must always have known. Even so, Luke found it hard to understand how Keeya could have come to mean the world to him in a matter of weeks. It was rather overwhelming to think of how his life and understanding of the world could have changed in such a short time. That young boy, playing on the rocks in Cornwall, seemed a stranger to him. Even his beloved parents and home were like a dream. The realisation scared him and he concentrated on sending his nightly message of hope to his parents, clinging to their memory as if it were an anchor, holding him fast to his humanity.

8
THE ISLAND

Luke felt a great deal of nervous anticipation the next day. He was not quite sure what kind of lessons to expect. Although Merya was gentle and approachable he found Tiyan as intimidating as Coryan had been.

After breakfast they ventured out into the warm shallows, to a natural circle of rocks that were cushioned with sea plants. It was so shallow that the top of Tiyan's large head emerged slightly above the water. The four of them rested there, enjoying the warmth of the sun on their shoulders. Luke and Keeya looked expectantly at their teachers. It was Tiyan who began.

'Luke, in order for you to become human again it is important to remember what being human means. What your body feels like, the way you think and everything that will re-forge your link with your humanity. And Keeya, listen carefully to everything that Luke describes, for not only will it help your own ability to transform, you need to know all you can about humans and the way they live and think in order to help them.'

Keeya leaned eagerly forward, wanting to hear and understand all about Luke's life as a human. Luke closed his eyes, trying to forget how natural it felt to be part of the sea. He began focusing his mind on his parents. He pictured his mother. He thought of the way she often ran her fingers through her short, brown hair whenever she felt impatient or was deep in thought. He pictured her frown lines and freckled skin, her smiles and the way she pulled and tousled his hair when she wanted to show him affection. He deliberately opened his mind to share these visions with his companions.

'What is her name?' asked Keeya.

'Karenza.' He smiled, as it felt funny to think of his mother as anything other than simply 'Mum'.

'She has your eyes, Luke. Is she kind?'

He laughed.

'Yes, when she isn't shouting at me for ruining my school shoes, forgetting my homework or coming home late from surfing.'

Keeya was puzzled.

'Does she love you?'

'Oh yes, she even shouts at me because she loves me. And she doesn't always shout, she often sings, and laughs, and she listens to me when I'm worried about things.'

His thoughts became almost too painful, thinking of his mum and how awful it must be for her, wondering if he was lost to her forever. He swallowed hard. Then Luke began describing his dad, the cancer that his dad had endured and how they hoped it had been cured. Luke spoke of the surfboard they had built together. Again, it was painful to think of his dad but lovely too. He talked about the things they did together, how large and cheerful his dad was, how brave and kind. Once Luke had mastered his emotions he began to enjoy talking of his human life, describing his nan and grandad, his friends at school, the things they were taught and the things they did for fun.

Keeya clung to every word, her eyes glowing with pleasure. Some human things confused her though.

'Luke, why do humans wrap everything in plastic? Is it really noisy, having to speak through your mouth instead of your mind? How do you all manage to hear and understand each other? Why do you use poisons to grow your food, does it not make you ill? What are the land animals like? Why do some stay in fields and houses? Do they like it? Why do you make machines to carry you across land, can you not walk and run on land, as we Eeshu can swim across our seas?'

Luke could not even begin to answer her questions and Merya intervened, laughing at her niece,

'Keeya, these are all good questions, but one at a time, please!'

Next, Luke was quizzed as to how he would be spending his time were he at home and what a normal day would be like. Luke tried to work out what time of year it must be and with a shock realised that it must be close to Christmas time. He tried to explain what Christmas was and who Jesus and Father Christmas were, but the Eeshu nodded knowingly.

'Yes, we have heard of the prophet Jesus. He has been mentioned in Eeshu histories as well as land histories.'

Luke then went on to describe the school carol concert, nativity play, Christmas trees and decorations, present giving and Christmas dinner. Though it seemed another world away he still felt that glow of Christmas magic experienced by every child who has ever enjoyed Christmas. Keeya was enchanted with the whole idea and suggested that they hold a similar celebration.

It was mid-afternoon by the time they finished their first lesson and Luke felt closer to his parents than he had for a long time, just by talking about them and remembering special things about them. He had also enjoyed telling Keeya all about his friends and life on land and she continued to ask him questions throughout the rest of the day, until finally he had to protest, laughing.

'Enough, Keeya. Let's have a quick swim and explore these reefs before supper. I want to enjoy the last of the sunshine before it fades.'

The next day they tried to create an underwater version of a Christmas celebration, starting by decorating the reef home with shells and stones. They found some driftwood which became their tree and they hung it with garlands of sea plants.

Luke tried to teach Keeya some carols but she interrupted all the time to question him about the words and she giggled too much. Luke became impatient with her and gave up.

After lunch they held a Gathering. Luke welcomed his spiritual friends, the Wise Ones, into his mind. He now realised he could call on them for help in his task and asked them to give comfort to his grieving family. He pictured his parents having Christmas without him. The need to be with his mum and dad and to enjoy a normal Christmas was overwhelming.

Keeya had liked the idea of a Father Christmas who gave gifts to children. Luke and Keeya decided to give each other a present too. They fashioned rings for each other out of twined plastic that Keeya had kept stored in her bag and they set polished crystals and coral into them. The rings were then sealed with juice from a sea plant and dried out in the sunshine. The rings set hard as rock. Luke and Keeya were delighted with their handy work and were impatient to wear their gifts.

Tiyan and Merya gave each of the children a precious healing crystal. Keeya was given a deep blue crystal that matched her eyes, whilst Luke received a green crystal. It had an inner fire of light trapped inside. Just to hold it and gaze at it made him feel powerful.

The following days continued with more lessons. The four of them would gather beneath the reef or out in the deep amongst the floating seaweed mats, or wherever seemed a peaceful place to listen and learn. Prompted by searching questions from Keeya, Merya and Tiyan, Luke found his own understanding of his land world challenged. He was often unable to answer their questions. He was after all only a child and he didn't really understand how his country was governed or why human beings lived as they did and why they treated the land and sea so selfishly.

Finally, Tiyan announced that it was time for Luke to practice transformation into human form. Luke was relieved. He was impatient to achieve transformation as soon as possible so that he could return home, tell his parents he was alive and then begin his dual life in the sea and on land. He could not wait.

Luke was expecting to pull himself out of the water then attempt to master his breathing as soon as possible. Instead he was frustrated to be told by Tiyan that first he and Keeya must meditate and imagine being a human. They also needed to think about why they wanted to be human before they even attempted transformation on land. Tiyan made them meditate all morning and Luke struggled to concentrate. He was impatient to see what he could do this time. He was sure he could transform easily now.

At last, Tiyan was satisfied that they were ready. He led them to the top of the reef where it joined with the tiny island. There was a gap in the reef, a shallow sandy patch on which they could comfortably stand with their bodies under water but with their faces raised above the surface. The minute Luke's face was in the open air he felt the burning rays of the sun on his skin and the warm gentle breeze on his face. He found he could master his breathing with more success than before. He looked at Keeya and saw that she too was relaxed and smiling. What a relief, not to have to experience that agony of struggling for breath. Perhaps Tiyan had been right to prepare them in this way after all.

Once breathing air became comfortable, Luke found it was easy to remember how to be human. He could feel subtle changes in his body. Cautiously, he began to walk slowly out of the reef and onto the dry, coral-pink sand of the islet. His skin prickled with the dry heat. The glare of the sun hurt his eyes but to be walking on land and breathing air again as a human being was thrilling. He wanted to shout in triumph.

Tiyan and Merya emerged gracefully from the sea, their bodies altering seamlessly as they walked onto dry land. Luke gazed at them in admiration. Tiyan then said,

'Come and sit beneath the trees, and we will rest and contemplate our surroundings.'

They all walked thankfully into the shade of some shrubs and trees. Keeya exclaimed at the beauty of a scarlet flower she found there. Her aunt threaded the bloom into Keeya's white hair and when everyone was settled and quiet Tiyan continued the lesson.

'Now that we are in human form we must become comfortable with our bodies. We must be aware of how it feels to breathe air, how the sand feels beneath our feet and how the breeze feels on our skin. The more details we can memorize now, the easier it will be the next time we transform. We can alter our bodies through our thought, our memory and our imagination.'

They all sat and concentrated, breathing and tasting the air that teased their drying white hair and noting the sensations of their human bodies. They listened to the wonderful sounds made by the birds and insects surrounding them. It was such a soothing spot that Luke was convinced he had discovered paradise. How strange to be in human form again! He looked down at his hands and feet, still encrusted with coral sand. There was barely any trace of webbing. He glanced at Keeya, marvelling at how strange she looked in human form. With her long white hair, her narrow face and huge dark eyes she still had something other-worldly about her. It was a fragile and elusive quality that no human possessed. How did he appear to her? She immediately heard this thought and responded,

'Your hair is darkening, but you still have something Eeshu about you that I can recognise. I wonder what your parents would think if they saw you now?'

Luke was alarmed to think he would appear freakish to other human beings but Tiyan interrupted their conversation.

'Luke has undergone a profound change since he became Eeshu and we cannot expect him to immediately regain his full human form as before. You two must come here every day until Luke has fully regained his human appearance.'

And so the days passed. Luke and Keeya emerged each day onto their small beach, breathing air as naturally as sea water. They explored the small island and discovered its rich array of birds, lizards and insects as well as plants and flowers. Keeya was thrilled at the beauty she found on land. Happiness made her glow. It created an aura around her that was reminiscent of her Eeshu glow beneath the sea.

In the early morning they would play happily together and behave as children should, the cares of the world temporarily forgotten. Luke introduced Keeya to the simple joy of building sandcastles, which they decorated with shells. Then when the day became too warm they would laze beneath the shade of a tree, holding hands whilst Luke told Keeya more stories of his life on land.

Sometimes, with his eyes half closed against the sun, Luke could see other small forms and energies that glowed around the living things that surrounded them. The trees had a restful energy, slow and wise, whilst the birds and insects had energy fields about them that crackled with impatience.

Their secret island was not as secret as they thought, however. Occasionally their peaceful contemplation would be shattered by the engines of boats which carried tourists and fishermen to the rich coral reefs. Far off out to sea they would spy huge ships, glimmering on the distant horizon. On these occasions the children would scramble for cover behind the trees and bushes, disturbed by the intrusion. Sometimes Luke wondered what would happen if he were discovered and taken away, back to his home in England. The thought filled him with panic. He was not ready yet to leave this paradise and his blissful days with Keeya. As much as he longed for eventual reunion with his family he knew that his present joyful experience would be lost, perhaps forever, and he was not yet ready to let it go.

Occasionally, Tiyan and Merya would join them on the island. The prophets appeared relaxed and comfortable in their human form. When a boat passed nearby, instead of running for cover or diving back into the sea they would wave casually at the people on the boat, who cheerfully waved back to them. Luke was not able to be so casual. His heart was pounding in case someone should recognise him. After all, he had now regained his original human appearance. His hair was now as dark as Keeya's was white. Keeya also felt tense in the presence of the human beings. Her last encounter, when she had tried to forage for human food, had been too traumatic. She would grip Luke's hand tightly until the boats had passed from sight.

Now that Luke was comfortable in both human and Eeshu form, Merya told him it was time to experience transformation into dolphin form. She explained to him,

'In an evolutionary sense, to return to dolphin form would be a step backwards. However, if you can achieve transformation into dolphin form as well, it would be a step forward in your understanding of the natural world around you.'

Keeya now became Luke's teacher as she was already adept at dolphin transformation. They would search out dolphin groups in the surrounding area and spend the day with them, hunting, playing and trying to communicate with them. The dolphins seemed to enjoy their company though they were initially alarmed when Luke threw himself onto the back of one and clung on when it tried to swim away. Keeya had told him it was the best way to understand the rhythm of a dolphin's movement.

Keeya would sometimes show off by changing from Eeshu to dolphin form and back again in a few moments. Luke was deeply envious of the natural ease with which she was able to transform herself. Then one day, without even consciously doing so, he found himself leaping out of the water with a dolphin tail in place of his legs. He felt such a sense of achievement. It raised his spirits so high that he could not stop leaping and diving in his new dolphin body for the rest of the day. Something about being in dolphin form made him feel more joyful than ever. He decided dolphins had to be the happiest animals on Earth.

Despite Luke's success in both forms of transformation, Tiyan insisted that Luke and Keeya continue to spend their days either as humans or dolphins for at least another week or so. One aspect that always surprised Luke was that his mind remained unchanged whichever form he took. He always had a strong sense of who he was, though the physical sensation and his abilities changed with each transformation.

Finally, Tiyan deemed it time for a new form of lesson.

'Luke, although you are accustomed to mind-communication I want you to master a more advanced control of your thoughts and the way in which you communicate. Your first task is to increase the distance at which you can continue conversation with Keeya, without asking the Wise Ones to assist you. Keeya will head in one direction and you will travel in the opposite direction. I want you to continue to link with each other until you lose all contact. You have never been physically very far apart so you do not yet know what your range of communication is.'

Luke was keen to find out. It had never occurred to him before that there might be a physical limit to the distance that thought-communication was possible. He had assumed it was infinite. At first it seemed that no amount of distance could diminish the clarity of their communication. They continued to chat easily, and relay images to each other of everything they were seeing. They felt so close, even though they were travelling further and further apart. Luke imagined how things might be. He could be in human form, living with his family but still able to hold Keeya close in his thoughts.

Gradually the images became less clear and by nightfall he could still hear Keeya but he really had to concentrate hard to understand her. Then he lost all communication with her. Luke realised for the first time since his drowning how very alone he was. In all his time in the sea he had always been in company and now he was not only alone in unfamiliar waters but it was dark and rather frightening. He wanted to return as quickly as possible to the reef cave, so he decided to transform into dolphin form. It was a much quicker and less tiring way to travel. At times he could sense large ships nearby and moved as far from their dangerous bulk as he could. At last, he heard both Keeya and Tiyan calling to him and they guided him back to the cave. He returned, feeling exhausted and disturbed by his experience of loneliness.

After that day Tiyan and Merya set Luke all kinds of tasks, training him to attune to other Eeshu within the area by meditation. He was pleased to establish a mental connection with Oreeya and then with another group of Eeshu out in deeper waters beyond the Sargasso Sea. After a great deal of practice he found it possible to link up simultaneously with several Eeshu in different locations, orchestrated by Tiyan or Merya. It reminded him of the satellite links used on news programmes, beaming images of reporters from different parts of the world. In fact the more Luke thought about it, the more he realised how like a television his mind was, with different channels available to view on demand. Luke soon learnt another valuable lesson, which was how to switch off that mental television. He found that if he kept his mind permanently open to receiving all incoming voices and images, it not only drained his energy but left him craving peace and quiet.

The next stage of learning was to keep his mind still, quiet and completely empty. This he found the biggest challenge so far. The inquiring mind of a child is never still. In his eagerness to learn about everything around him, Luke was easily distracted. The only way in which he could achieve mental stillness was at night, or sometimes when dozing on the island beneath the afternoon sun. He could be lulled into a trance-like state by the rhythmic brush of the waves on the shore and the steady hum of insects. He was never sure for how long he achieved an empty mind, for the next thing he knew he would be waking up from a heavy sleep.

Luke had now been living in the reef cave for many weeks and his learning experience had been so intense that he felt he had been there for an eternity. He could not imagine how it must feel to be Keeya and to have already existed for a hundred years, with hundreds of more years yet to live. The more he thought of it the more concerned he became for their future together. Keeya heard these thoughts in him. She said carefully,

'Luke, when you return to your family, do you think you will still want to live as an Eeshu too? I wonder, for surely it must elongate your life, but I don't know how your family would feel if you kept leaving them.'

Luke looked down, staring blindly at his hands. He was feeling more and more anxious about his future.

'I was thinking perhaps I could spend daytime at home and school, then my time off and weekends living with you as an Eeshu. I don't know how it works. I don't want to cause any more grief to my parents but when I'm grown up I will be able to choose how I live. I will come back to live in the sea a lot more often. That will surely mean I can live longer, though perhaps not as long as your lifetime will be.'

A worried silence fell over them. Though the future prayed on their minds, neither felt able to discuss it with Tiyan or Merya. The question of Luke's immediate future, however, inevitably had to be discussed. Now that winter was coming to an end so were the lessons. One day Tiyan called the children to him. When they were dutifully seated in front of him he frowned, looking grave.

'Luke, you are almost ready to return to your human existence. Merya and I have prepared you as best we can for your future role. We have been told, however, that in order to complete your education you must make your final journey across the ocean alone.'

The children gasped, horrified.

'But uncle, surely I will travel back with Luke and then return to my own home?' Keeya asked, looking anxiously at Tiyan.

He shook his head.

'No Keeya, you must remain here, for we have more to teach you. You now have the responsibility of a community leader, a role you have inherited from your grandfather. Now that Luke is practised in transformation and thought-communication he has one more important lesson to learn. It is not a lesson that can be taught by myself or Merya.'

The children were upset. They had not realised they would be parted so soon. Then Tiyan continued,

'However, before Luke leaves us there is still some guidance that I can give to you both, to help you on your life's journey. Firstly, I want to show you how to cope with your burden, to show you that you can achieve all that is being asked of you.'

The children were distracted from their sorrow when, with a slight gesture of his wrist, Tiyan created a huge spinning globe of water in front of them. The globe was a perfect replica of Earth, with all its seas and landmasses in perfect detail. Luke looked at the scale of it and wondered how he could possibly save that enormous planet, full of billions of humans, Eeshu, animals and plants. He wanted to run away from the enormous task being thrust upon him. It seemed hopeless.

Tiyan then reduced the huge globe into a small revolving ball which he threw to Luke. Though made of water it felt solid in Luke's hands. As he grasped the world within in his hand the watery replica of planet Earth became so small that he could hold it pinched between his thumb and forefinger.

'That is the size of the problem. With the power of your thought alone, the problems of the world can be reduced to something as small as this. Whenever you feel overwhelmed by the size of the problem, imagine it reduced to the size of a pebble and you will achieve your goals.'

'Tiyan, what exactly are the problems that I must help humans overcome? I know there is a problem with rubbish, and fishing, and chemicals being washed into the sea, but I don't see how a boy like me can do anything about it.' Luke looked at Tiyan with a worried expression.

At this point Merya joined in the discussion.

'Many humans are like children who have a whole basket of sweets in front of them. They grab all the sweets they can and gorge on them. They do so, even knowing it will make them sick and knowing there will be no sweets left once they have eaten them all. Yet still they cannot seem to stop themselves. That is how it seems to the Eeshu, when humans grab more and more creatures from the sea, without thinking if any will be left for future generations to come.'

'But what can I do about it?' asked Luke helplessly.

Both Tiyan and Merya smiled at him.

'You will help change human attitudes and understanding. You can influence the minds of human beings and help them to nurture the world instead of stripping it of all resources. You will persuade them to love their planet and take care of it. Then nature will repair itself. We Eeshu have many ideas for recovering and recycling all the plastic rubbish in our oceans. We have preserved plants and creatures in order to reintroduce any that are made extinct and when humans stop pouring poisons into the seas we can help to heal the damage.'

Merya looked at the bewildered boy and put her arm around him.

'Do not worry, Luke, you are still a child and all this is in your future. When the time is right you will be able to achieve all that is necessary, but that time is not now. Remember all that you have learned so far and the rest of your life's journey will unfold naturally and happily.'

Keeya and Luke looked anxiously at each other, scared by their future adult responsibilities. They felt sad that their blissful time here on the island was about to end forever. However much Tiyan and Merya tried to reassure them, the children knew their lives together would never be the same again.

On the eve of Luke's departure from this tropical paradise, he and Keeya sat on the beach with their legs bathed in seawater. It had become amusing to them to partially transform their bodies, one half in human form and the other half in Eeshu form. At this moment they sat comfortably in the shallows, human from the waist up and breathing air with human lungs, but with webbed feet and legs that were soft with rubbery, pearlescent Eeshu skin. Although they felt heartbroken at the thought of being parted they found it hard to talk about. Instead they sat in silence, their floating Eeshu legs being nudged by the waves.

Finally Keeya gave a deep sigh.

'Promise me you will contact me every day, at sunset, to tell me that you are safe and to let me know what you have been doing.'

Luke nodded.

'Yes of course, as long as I can. I can't believe that I'm finally going back home to my parents. I don't even know what to tell them, how to explain where I've been, how I've survived. I suppose I'd better come up with a convincing story.'

Keeya frowned.

'Can you not just tell them the truth?'

Luke shook his head.

'They will think I'm mad, or making it up. I don't want to lie, but in this case it is for the best. Maybe one day I will be able to tell Mum and Dad the truth. I don't know. Maybe one day they could meet you, and then they would have to believe me!'

There was another thoughtful silence, then Luke said,

'To be honest, the thing I'm most worried about is travelling back on my own. It's such a long way, and without your guidance I'm scared of getting lost.'

Keeya gave his arm a reassuring squeeze.

'Do not worry. There is a line of volcanic mountains which runs all the way up the centre of the Atlantic Ocean. Part of this mountain range lies close to your home coastline. It is mostly all beneath the surface, but in some places, at its highest peaks, it emerges above the sea to form islands. You can always find food, shelter and Eeshu communities along the way, and with help from the Wise Ones you will never be alone or without guidance.'

'I suppose so', said Luke, but his stomach churned with nerves. He was not looking forward to his departure in the morning, or of being alone in the vast ocean. But most of all he dreaded being without his soul mate, Keeya.

9
THE DEEP

Despite feeling sick with nerves, Luke put on a brave face as he said goodbye to the prophets. Then with a regretful backward glance at the homely cave he set off with Keeya. She had insisted on travelling with him as far as the abyss, which lay on the outer edge of the Sargasso Sea. From here he would begin his solo journey across the Atlantic Ocean.

Keeya and Luke had been swimming for only a short time when they were joined unexpectedly by Oreeya and her family. The sorrowful departure that Luke had been dreading became instead a cheerful party, lifting his spirits and courage enormously.

It was a glorious morning, with the scent of spring approaching. In a moment of high spirits the Eeshu decided to transform into dolphins and they leapt and played as they escorted Luke. He felt his spirits rise and when they reached the indigo waters of the abyss, he turned to his cheery companions and thanked them for their support. They wished him good luck, waved goodbye and then left him alone with Keeya.

For their final goodbye Luke and Keeya reverted back to Eeshu form, holding hands and looking shyly at each other.

'Promise me you will keep in contact every sunset, just to let me know how you are,' said Keeya, looking fiercely at Luke and trying to control her trembling lips.

Luke swallowed back the lump in his throat.

'Of course I will. Well, wish me luck. I'll see you again as soon as possible, once I've had a chance to settle back into human life.'

They held hands briefly, then their grasp slipped loose and Luke looked apprehensively out to the dark blue waters of the deep ocean. Conscious of Keeya's anxious eyes on him he bravely surged forward. In his effort to appear confident and strong he managed to quell the nerves of embarking on his solo journey. Before long Keeya was out of sight and he was truly, utterly alone.

He knew that he had to cross a great expanse before he reached the underwater mountain range that was his pathway home. Tiyan had explained to him that the mountains had been formed when the continents of America, Africa and Europe had been split apart millions of years ago, leaving a ridge of submerged volcanic mountains. This underwater mountain range divided the Atlantic Ocean from south to north. By following it Luke could be sure that he would eventually reach the sea near to his home, which he would recognise by its taste and sounds. When Tiyan had explained all this, it had seemed so simple that Luke felt slightly reassured. But first he must cross an abyss, a body of water so deep that it seemed like endless night beneath him.

Just as Luke was considering taking dolphin form to make his journey easier and faster, he heard a voice calling his name. It was not Keeya's voice however, it was a low voice that vibrated through his body and froze his blood. Hoping he had just imagined the voice, he continued onwards, looking nervously beneath him. He saw a vague movement deep below him so he hurried forward, trying to cross this abyss as quickly as he could. The voice echoed in his head, stronger and more insistently. His heart beat faster and he tried to ignore the voice summoning him down into the midnight below him.

'Luke, answer them!' boomed an angry voice in his head, a

voice which sounded just like Coryan's. Luke shook his head in confusion and looked around him. There was nothing. He cautiously swam onwards then became aware of someone swimming alongside him. He slowly turned his head. The huge form of Coryan was swimming next to him. Luke felt both happy to see his old protector and abashed that he had made him angry. The mighty Eeshu pointed downwards to the depths then dissolved back into the foam.

Luke stopped and looked downwards. He felt shamed by Coryan's anger at him for ignoring the call of the Deep Eeshu. But there was a horror that filled him whenever he saw those dark and forbidding creatures. Also, he feared the black depths of the ocean and the hideous and dangerous creatures that lurked unseen beneath him. He was thousands of miles away from the monster that had devoured Coryan but his fear of it was intensified by his feeling of vulnerability in these strange, lonely waters.

Luke took the green crystal from his bag and stared into its fiery depths. A warm courage slowly filled him as he felt the power of the crystal over him. With a steely determination he dived downwards, following the call of the Deep Eeshu. The deeper he swam the darker and colder the water became. The water pressure on his lungs and head became unbearable. He had to pause, trying to meditate himself into a more comfortable physical state in which he could cope with the great pressure of the depths. In the darkness his special Eeshu light was pale and sad compared with the amazing creatures that illuminated the black water. The creatures in the deep were mostly of transparent jelly but their forms were so varied and bizarre and their bioluminescence so dazzling in colour and brightness, that some of his apprehension turned to wonder at their alien beauty. However, this unexpected beauty was balanced by ugliness. Just as his vision would be lit by some dazzling display, out of the darkness a grotesque and sinister fish would emerge. And as Luke reluctantly sank lower, his head and body aching under the intense pressure, the creatures became larger and more terrifying. Giant squid the size of ships would pass nearby, their long tentacles reaching forward for prey and unseen things would brush past him, making him cringe in horror.

Luke also found the extreme cold hard to bear. This morning he had swum in deliciously warm water and now he was sinking into depths that sunlight could not reach. The water was as icy as the Arctic seas.

'Why do the Deep Eeshu choose to live somewhere so awful?' Luke wondered to himself.

'Because it can also be wonderful. It is virtually untouched by humans and it holds the secrets of our very existence.'

Luke gasped, for the voice was so close to him. Straining to see in the gloom, Luke watched three male Eeshu drift up to him from the blackness. The tallest nodded gravely to Luke, his large black eyes staring hard at the boy.

'Welcome light traveller, my name is Goryan and I am the leader of our community here. Come with us, we have much to tell you.'

Despite his suspicion of the Deep Eeshu, Luke was nevertheless glad of their company and protection. He followed them willingly; curious to see how they lived down in the forgotten depths. Now that his eyes had adjusted to the darkness, he could see that they had reached the craggy foothills at the base of a sea mountain. There was a green phosphorescent light that lit up this part of the seabed, the source seeming to come from the mountain itself. The sea floor here was covered with boulders and debris. Some of it moved when stepped on, revealing giant, flat fish that slurped greedily on all the dead matter that had sunk to the bottom.

As they drew nearer, Luke could see caves that were hollowed into the volcanic rock of the mountainside. He recognised them as the traditional style of Eeshu homes, with their open front rooms. The green light that lit this dreary community came from a type of luminous green algae that carpeted the rocks around the caves.

To his relief Luke found that the temperature here felt warmer and Goryan pointed to the streams of boiling water that leaked out from cracks in the sea floor. Around these vents in the volcanic rock were thousands of tiny shrimps, feasting on its tasty minerals. To Luke the water smelt awful, like bad eggs. In fact he found the outside world of the Eeshu community here a bleak and strange place in which to live. Their cave homes though were surprisingly cosy, even luxuriously furnished. The entrance room that he was taken to by his companions was full of books and scrolls and the walls were decorated with some astonishing pictures of both sea and land people. Goryan gestured to Luke to sit down.

'Luke, you are here to finally unlock the mystery of the Eeshu race and their history. In doing so you will understand your own human race and you will understand what can be done to save this ancient world of ours. Firstly, however, you must be hungry and tired, for I know that the atmosphere down here is difficult for you to tolerate and you will need some time to adjust. This plant may help you.'

Goryan then passed a slimy, blue plant to Luke, on which the boy reluctantly nibbled. It had a sharp flavour to it. Almost immediately Luke felt relief from the water pressure as his lung capacity expanded and he felt himself become lighter.

'And how is the lovely Keeya? We miss her very much, for she is a child that touches all of our hearts.'

Luke was surprised.

'You miss her? Did she stay here then?' He looked around him, trying to imagine her here.

'She did not tell you her history? When her mother was killed trying to rescue her, she remained with us for a few years whilst her father tried to cope with his grief. His spirit was not as strong and forgiving as Keeya's is. Although Keeya was a mere baby at the time her light touched us all.'

'What did her mother rescue her from? What killed her?' Suddenly it seemed very important to know.

'That which killed her grandfather and hunted you all in the ice. That ancient creature tried to feast on Keeya, and so her mother sacrificed herself instead to save her daughter.'

Even as he heard these terrible words Luke realised the truth of it. The visions of that hideous reptilian face and its terrifying teeth made him feel faint with horror. So that explained the jagged scarring on Keeya's knee.

'Why does it want to hunt us? There are so many other things, larger than us, to feed on.'

'It hungers for your light. Those whose spirit is strongest become its prey.' Goryan then continued, 'That creature was bred by the land people of Atlantis, our ancestors. They were given the knowledge of creating life, to add to the wonderful abundance that had been created for them. Unfortunately some used their knowledge to experiment for their own purposes. Ancient species were recreated, like that dinosaur that hunted you and also diseases and savage beasts. They even created the Eeshu through their relationship with the wild and innocent sea nymphs that guarded the oceans at that time. The legacy of Atlantis still remains on this Earth and your current human species is following their example and committing the same mistakes.'

'If that dinosaur was created by the people of Atlantis, thousands of years ago, how can it still be alive? Are there more?'

'Each time it feeds on the light of an Eeshu its cells are renewed and the creature is reborn. It will never die as long as it can feed on the Eeshu. Fortunately the foolish Atlanteans created only that one dinosaur, for they soon realised their terrible mistake.'

Luke shuddered with horror at the thought of the monster. It was indestructible, it would live forever. It would always be out there, ready to hunt him and devour him, or Keeya, or any of his Eeshu friends. The idea was so awful that Luke tried to distract himself with other thoughts.

'Where was Atlantis? Does it still exist?' Luke asked, fascinated by Goryan's words.

Goryan gave a wry smile and shook his head.

'Yes and no. Atlantis was the continent that covered this planet before the fire in the heart of the Earth rose up to the surface and splintered the land apart, creating new oceans and continents. The knowledge and legacy of those first people were divided between these new continents and thousands of years later new civilisations were created by their descendants in South America, Babylon, Egypt, Greece, China and India.' Goryan gestured at the pictures surrounding them on the cave walls. 'See, these pictures show the civilisations that became dominant on land. They all had the light of knowledge and the choice of how to use it. They have all now passed on from this ageing Earth, back to the Source.'

'What is the Source?' asked Luke. This was the most curious history lesson he had ever had.

Goryan smiled at him.

'You already know, you have been there, in the heavens and in the light. The Source is the light; it is our home, our father and mother. It is love and life. It is what we are made from and the place to where we will always return.'

'You mean, God?' asked Luke hesitantly, remembering the disembodied voice that spoke to him in the cradle of light.

'That is a word and concept that humans have created. Now Luke, I will leave you to your rest. Sleep well.'

Goryan gravely nodded his head to the boy then departed, leaving Luke to mull over the astonishing truths that the Deep Eeshu had explained to him.

Luke had been given a comfortable chamber in which to sleep and as he gratefully curled up in the bed he thought of his beloved Keeya, growing up as a tiny child down here in the depths. No wonder that she was so trusting of these dark, mysterious Deep Eeshu.

'Luke, can you hear me? Are you well?' It was as if Keeya had heard his thoughts about her.

'Keeya, yes! I'm here with Goryan, down in the deep. He told me that you lived here as a baby. It's all a bit, well, gloomy down here. But your grandfather swam beside me and told me I must visit them here, and Goryan has told me some interesting things. How about you? Did you visit the island today?'

'Yes, but it seemed so lonely without you. I am going to travel home before summer arrives, shall we meet up then?'

'Yes! I would love my family to meet you. Well, goodnight and I'll speak to you tomorrow.'

'Goodnight Luke. Send my love to Goryan.'

Luke spent the next few days amongst the Deep Eeshu. He found them solemn but not sinister as he had first thought. In fact they showed him great kindness in their slow, serious fashion. The Eeshu children were fascinated by Luke. They found the idea of living on land and breathing air strange and wonderful. These dark and serious children eagerly showed him around their homes that nestled amongst the glowing green boulders.

Luke discovered that the green algae was an important food source for both the Eeshu here and the bizarre sea creatures which thrived down in the dark, even without sunlight. He also learnt that living down in these depths could be very dangerous. The lower slopes of the mountain were split with deep cracks and Luke could not resist poking about them, exploring and looking for treasure, just as he used to do along the cliffs of Cornwall. Within the cracks there were seams of glittering stones, those fiery crystals which emitted their own light. Luke wanted to excavate some from the unyielding rock, to take back as a gift for his parents but he had no tools. Instead, he continued to search amongst the rock, seeking any loose stones that he could take with him.

On one occasion he found a wide, shallow crack which ended in a small cave. Cautiously, he climbed down into the crack and felt his way forward, hoping to find treasures hidden within the cave. Behind him he heard a warning cry from the Eeshu children that followed him everywhere. Puzzled, Luke turned round then screamed in shock when two giant, fleshy tentacles rolled out of the cave and wrapped tightly around his arm. Luke pulled against the grasp of the tentacles but he could not stop himself from being dragged mercilessly towards a sharp beak. More tentacles flowed out, wrapping painfully about his body. Luke could do nothing but scream and writhe in terror, his arms locked by his sides. The bulbous head of a giant octopus ballooned out from the cave and the creature opened its beak, ready to devour Luke. He strained away from the sharp beak which snapped at him, ready to bite his head off. Realising he was about to die, Luke closed his eyes against the final horror. Suddenly he felt a painful jolt through his body and the crushing tentacles relaxed around him. He fell, shaking, onto his knees. Desperately he scrambled away from the octopus, his body shuddering uncontrollably. Luke saw one of the Eeshu children prod the giant octopus with a crystal rod that sent an electric current into the creature. The octopus shrank away, folding its enormous bulk back into its hiding place.

Luke collapsed into the arms of his rescuers, shaking like a jelly with shock, both at the horror of almost being dinner for an enormous octopus and from the electrical charge that had stunned his attacker and himself at the same time.

After that horrific incident Luke chose to stay close to the cave homes and their gardens. It seemed that plants could grow without light here, for there was an abundance of nutrients on the ocean floor, although the plants had little colour or flavour. He began to yearn for sunlight, for warmth and for colour and he missed his days on the paradise island with Keeya. The only thing he really liked down in the perpetual darkness was the wondrous displays of light and patterns created by the myriad of jelly-like creatures that lit the dark waters around them. The variety and complexity of these bioluminescent creatures was infinite. Their beauty would distract him for a while but then Luke's thoughts would return to the terrifying monster that was waiting for him out in that darkness, ready to strike when he was alone and vulnerable.

Despite the danger, Luke could not bear to stay down in the deep forever. He longed to get his lessons over and done with and continue his journey home. He spent most of his time with Goryan, who had taken on the role of Luke's teacher. He showed Luke the wealth of books and scrolls collected from all ages, although the writing was incomprehensible to Luke. Or at least so it seemed at first glance.

One day the lessons took a more interesting turn when Goryan was showing Luke yet another scroll of curious pictures of ancient and strange animals that had once lived on Earth.

'Can you understand this writing, Luke?' asked Goryan in his slow deep voice.

'No! I can't read any of these old writings.' Luke was puzzled by the question, for surely Goryan knew Luke didn't know any ancient languages.

'Look again child. Connect with your Wise Ones and see what is revealed to you.'

Luke was unsure but did as he was told. He asked his mysterious spiritual friends for help and then stared at the incomprehensible scribbles in front of him. Slowly but surely a meaning became clear from the strange symbols.

'I can understand the writing, I think. But how can I read its meaning?'

'Because you have read it before, in another lifetime. This is not your first visit to Earth, nor your last. Close your eyes and ask the Wise Ones to reveal the truth to you.'

Luke dutifully closed his eyes and waited for his history to be revealed to him. Swiftly his mind was taken to a beautiful garden and at its centre he could see a fountain, built in the form of a pyramid. Luke saw men and women, dressed in loose robes, strolling through gardens that were filled with exotic and strange plants. There were children playing and chasing amongst marble statues. Others relaxed in cool, quiet buildings. Luke looked down and saw his own feet in sandals, a kind of pen and a scroll in his hand as if he had just been writing. Luke was so surprised to see this vision that he lost his mental connection and the vision disappeared. He looked in astonishment at Goryan.

The Eeshu nodded his head sagely, as if he had shared the vision with Luke.

'Luke, like many others on Earth, you have lived in Atlantis and in other ages of mankind. Each new lifetime that you experience on Earth leaves its mark on you, leaving memories and knowledge that your soul stores inside of you.'

Luke shook his head in bewilderment. This was strange news to him.

123

'How come I can't remember lives that I've lived before? How can it be possible?'

Goryan looked at him deeply with his fathomless black eyes.

'We come to Earth in a new form when we want to learn new lessons and our past is there if we choose to access it. But our soul remains the same. The body we wear is simply the clothing for our soul.'

Luke found the whole idea disturbing and incredible. He was even more perturbed by Goryan's next words.

'The people of Atlantis were the first civilised people to live on this Earth but they came from a civilisation that was even older. They came to this Earth from another world entirely, bringing their knowledge with them as they began to populate this wonderful, bountiful planet. This Earth was a gift to them from the Source.'

Luke gave a snort of disbelief.

'You mean they were aliens?'

Goryan looked at him disapprovingly.

'There are more worlds, civilisations and timelines in this universe than humans can possibly imagine. Most of you are like children, imagining that the universe revolves around you, thinking that humans are the only intelligent form in existence. You look at the stars as children view the world. A child grows up and sees only the details near to him and thinks these details are the only truth. Mankind cannot see the world as a whole, nor can it see the whole truth. So it is that humans see only the tiniest part of the universe, the stars and planets around them and imagine themselves a significant part of it. You are specks of dust! And yet you are also a vital part of the universe. One day humankind will comprehend this truth.'

'You don't like human beings, then?'

'On the contrary, it is our greatest wish to befriend them, to share knowledge and resources with them. But I am afraid we view humans as young children that are not wise enough to be responsible for the future of our planet. They have the intelligence but not the spiritual evolution to use their knowledge wisely.'

Goryan paused then said brusquely,

'Well Luke, that is all I have to tell you for now. Tomorrow, when you feel rested and ready, it will be time for you to continue your journey. Sleep well.'

Goryan then turned and moved majestically away, his long black hair floating like tentacles about his head. Luke was left feeling abashed. Had he been a bad pupil? He felt somehow his ignorance had offended his Eeshu teacher but it was pretty far-fetched stuff that Goryan had told him. Descended from aliens? Honestly. Still, Luke did have to admit to himself that since his drowning all those months ago, incredible things had happened and impossible things had turned out to be true. So why not be descended from an alien race?

Luke's lesson had exhausted him, so with a huge yawn he decided to go to bed. He snuggled down, then spoke briefly with Keeya about his day. When he fell asleep it was to dream of aliens, monsters and the stars.

10
JOURNEY'S END

Luke woke up suddenly, trying to drag his mind from the clutches of a hideous nightmare. In his dreams he had been trying to rescue Keeya from the monster when it had attacked him instead. He was screaming in agony but even worse was the realisation that he would never see Keeya or his parents again. That thought hurt him more than the jaws of the monster that had been ripping him apart.

Luke sat up, his heart pounding. He called out to Keeya for comfort and after a while he heard her anxiously responding to him. She sang a soothing song to him, so sweet and gentle that the horror of his nightmare gradually loosened its grip. He fell back into a calm and dreamless sleep.

He awoke once more in the perpetual darkness of the Deep. He was feeling weak from his disturbed night and his heart quailed at the thought of the dangers ahead. When Goryan saw him he must have realised how terrified Luke was of his forthcoming journey alone. He put his huge purple hand on the boy's shoulder in a gesture of comfort.

'Never fear, young light-bringer. Remember, the Wise Ones will protect you, for it is not your time to die. You have an important role yet to fulfil. We will escort you closer to the surface and guide you to the most suitable route for your onward journey.'

Goryan's words brought some comfort to Luke but the horror of loss that he had experienced in his nightmare still lingered. Then Luke asked a question that he had been longing to ask Goryan since he had woken up.

'Are the Wise Ones the alien people who established Atlantis? Or are they ghosts? Or Angels? I can never see their faces clearly, because they have too much light around them.'

'Some of the Wise Ones are beings who have lived on Earth and have gone back to their Source; others have never left the light of the Source. '

'Why do they want to help us?'

Goryan gave a rare smile.

'The Wise Ones love us and want us to live a happy and meaningful life. They are like parents and we are their children. They will always love us, whatever we do, and they will always help us whenever we ask them. Now, light traveller, it is time to leave.'

'Why do you call me a "light traveller"? '

'Luke, you have so many more lessons to learn and I cannot teach you everything. In time all your questions will be answered. Now follow me. My people and I will guide you safely to the surface and set you on your course.'

As Luke and his escorts rose higher out of the darkness, both the atmosphere and the water pressure lightened and Luke's spirits rose too. When he felt the first searching fingers of sunlight brush his skin he gave a sigh of relief. The beautiful blue of the water reflecting the sky above made him think of home, his final destination. With his escort of giant Deep Eeshu by his side Luke felt more confident and less anxious about his onward journey.

Goryan indicated the peaks of a mountain range beneath them.

'Luke, follow these peaks all the way to your colder waters in the north, but please be wary. These mountains are restless and can crack and move, throwing out magma and gases that can be very dangerous. There are some volcanic Eeshu communities along the way, so if ever you need help simply call out and someone will hear you. Never think you are alone. Good luck, Luke, it has been an honour to have met you.'

Luke thanked his Deep Eeshu friend and said goodbye, feeling ashamed of his previous unworthy thoughts about Goryan. Then Luke gazed below at the beautiful mountainside beneath him. It reminded him of the Alps, a glorious range of craggy peaks and ravines covered with plants, flowers, sponges and corals. Suddenly feeling quite hungry at the sight of all that delicious abundance he dived eagerly downwards, harvesting lush vegetation and beaming happily with the pleasure of being in the light once more.

Luke continued his journey northwards with greater optimism, taking the form of a dolphin and covering huge distances. At times he had schools of dolphins accompanying him, at other times he swam swiftly through the ocean alone. He was feeling excited at the idea of seeing his parents at last.

There were stretches along the mountain range that were still shifting and oozing magma, or hissing out black jets of water. It was both fascinating and alarming. Luke paused to watch a large fat snake of magma push its way up through the scar of rock and crawl slowly along the cracked mountain ravine. It looked like a fiery, undulating serpent, spitting and blackening as the magma cooled in the cold Atlantic waters. The noise and heat was terrifying and the gases made him gasp to breathe but Luke could not tear himself away from the sight.

He was shocked to see an Eeshu swimming dangerously close to this volcanic serpent. He swiftly reverted to Eeshu form and called out a warning. The Eeshu turned and waved calmly to him. It was a female Eeshu. She had smoky dark hair and red skin that echoed the magma rock cooling around her.

'Welcome Luke! Have a care not to get too close, and I will join you shortly when this eruption has calmed.'

Luke was now accustomed to being known already by the strangers he met. He hovered closer to the surface of the sea while he waited for this reckless Eeshu lady. After a while she swam up to meet with him.

'Luke, I have been waiting for you. But then this eruption occurred. It is necessary for me to attend the birth of any new land that is being created beneath us. I think we Volcanic Eeshu have the most thrilling task of all the Eeshu guardians, for we witness the birth and death of land, we see islands created and destroyed, and mountains raised or sunk back into the heart of our planet.'

She beamed happily at him.

'My name, by the way, is Areeya. I have been told to ensure your safety across this section of unpredictable mountains. You are so fortunate, young one! I have watched this process of creation and death thousands of times during my hundreds of years on this planet, but I never tire of it. Not only are new lands formed, but over millennia we have seen new seas created too.'

Luke smiled at this friendly and extraordinary lady.

'What exactly do you do Areeya, when you watch these lands being made? What are you guardian of?'

She looked at him in puzzlement.

'Why, my role is to be a witness. The new lands that are made, the land that is lost, all are recorded in my mind. That knowledge is then shared with all others. Inside my consciousness is the whole history of our planet, and I guard that knowledge.'

A thought occurred to Luke.

'Do you have a memory of the birth and destruction of Atlantis? I have seen a glimpse of Atlantis, but I would like to know more.'

'Ah, Atlantis, what a beautiful and abundant land that was! I was not alive to witness it, but I carry its memory in my mind. It was a land vibrant with creation. The people that came to live there were originally of the skies. They were so full of light that the sun paled in comparison. They built wonderful cities and filled them with elegant architecture and beautiful gardens. They helped to develop the plants, insects, birds and animals that thrived amongst them. Yes, the early years of their

existence here was a blissful and harmonious one.
Unfortunately, over time these beings of light and air became
heavy with the weight of this Earth and their minds began to
turn inwardly upon themselves. Shadows entered their hearts
and minds and they began to lose their connection with the
Wise Ones. Their beautiful lands became troubled and the
Earth began to shake as disharmony unbalanced this world.
Eventually the heart of the Earth boiled over and split Atlantis
apart, separating those that survived into small pockets of
communities living thousands of miles apart. But over time this
planet healed itself, allowing our wonderful oceans to soothe its
scars.'

'Wow, so there is no trace left of Atlantis on Earth? No piece
of land that they used to live on?'

Areeya paused, then cautiously nodded her head.

'Yes, there are traces of the land that used to be Atlantis,
north of here. But not as far as your home, Luke. However I do
not think that knowledge will be of use to you. There will be
another Chosen One whose task it is to reveal that truth.'

She paused, looking distant and pensive, as if her mind was
suddenly very far away. He thought she had forgotten him
entirely when she said unexpectedly,

'You know, it is strange that humans cannot see us. We are
all of us from the same source and our bodies are formed of the
same atoms. We are all made of water, minerals and chemicals,
just like the Earth that nourishes us. Do you suppose one day
all human beings will be able to see us, interact with us and
share our planet equally?'

Her question interested Luke but he never got the chance to
answer her, for with a brief smile and a wave she suddenly left
him. Clearly she had been distracted by other matters. With a
shrug Luke continued his journey, gliding over the mountain
peaks like an eagle, peering at the tiny plants and creatures
miles below him. Above him the Atlantic was becoming restless,
as if the skies and winds had been stirred in anger. He decided
to travel down deeper beneath the waves, trying to ride out
their forceful movements in the shelter of the mountainside. It

was also an opportune moment to harvest a meal. He found a wide ledge to rest on and enjoyed a varied selection of plants within easy reach. He was feeling quite tired by now and he could see by the fading light that it was time to find shelter and rest. The sea about him was churning and pulling at him and he realised it must be quite a violent storm above. He cautiously made his way down into a deeper crevasse, searching for a small cave in which to shelter. He did not much like it down here, for the water was colder and the plants and animals were sparser. Despite his recent stay in much deeper waters, he still found the darkness uncomfortable.

He checked about him for any giant octopus that might be lying in wait but there were only harmless sea creatures hiding in the nooks and crannies, more fearful of him than he was of them. A lone shark weaved past him but Luke had realised long ago that sharks posed no threat to him. Instead he enjoyed watching its stealthy progress until it was out of sight.

Luke could not find a safe and comfortable shelter so he decided to continue his journey until he found a cave, hopefully before the light faded completely. After another hour of searching he still had not found suitable shelter. The sea was getting uncomfortably rough. He headed slightly deeper and found a tough piece of fan coral to tie himself to, with the help of the buoyancy cord in his bag. It was unpleasant down in the darkness, so he felt in his bag for his crystals and drew comfort from them. He called out to Keeya. Now that the miles stretched between them her voice came through only faintly. They shared the events of their day and then said goodnight.

Even after Luke had said goodbye, he still wanted to maintain that precious contact with Keeya. He felt a presentiment that something terrible was about to happen and it made him feel anxious. He wanted the comfort of Keeya's voice in his head. Never had he felt so alone and vulnerable. With a sigh he tried to get some sleep but he felt too worried to relax and trust the ocean to look after him. Suddenly he felt the water shake around him. It had not been stirred by the winds above him but by something shaking deep below him. Rapidly untying himself from the coral he peered downwards. Was that a thin line of red far below him?

Luke cautiously swam lower and this time another tremor shook the whole mountainside, causing rocks and coral to tumble downwards. He realised at once that he was in danger of being crushed by falling rocks. He swam upwards, towards the faint glimmer of light near the surface. It was the soft light of the benign moon, remote from the turbulence happening deep beneath the waves. The seabed shifted, creaked and groaned and fiery red oozed up from the cracks. The boiling lava was trying to push its way out of the seabed, creating a small earthquake. At the surface Luke battled through the surging, stormy seas, trying to flee from the irritable seabed beneath him.

His sense of imminent danger lingered still. He struggled on for as long as possible through the storm but it sapped his strength. Soon he was too exhausted to continue. He noticed that the mountain peaks beneath him were higher and closer to the surface. Some peaks breached the water, forming small islets. Hoping to find some kind of shelter there, he explored one of the larger islets and felt a huge relief when he came across the mouth of an extinct volcano. The centre of the crater was submerged but a section of the crater edge rose out of the water like a wall, creating a lake of protected water. The crater was deep but its walls were rich with plants and corals.

Luke dived hopefully into it, finding relief within its calmer waters. He found a ledge where he was able to rest and recover, leaning his head wearily against a cushion of seaweed. His eyes closed and his tired mind began to gently swim away into darkness and peace. He must have fallen asleep but then a sense of danger penetrated his dreams. As his mind reluctantly left the comfort of rest, his senses became aware of another presence. A sinister and familiar groan made his eyes snap open in an instant. Could it be? No, please, not the monster. Luke listened tensely, his body rigid with fear. Another, louder moan issued up from the depths of the dormant volcano crater. Luke panicked, wondering if he should try to flee the water and climb onto land, or stay still in the hope that the monster would remain unaware of his presence.

No other sound came from the depths, no hideous face with lethal teeth appeared, ready to tear him to shreds. Had he imagined it? No, there was definitely something down there and he would not be safe if he remained. If he was going to escape this place he must leave now, whilst the monster was quiet and unaware of him.

Scarcely daring to breathe, Luke inched his way up the rock face, cutting his hand on some sharp coral and releasing a faint trail of blood into the water. He looked in horror at the blood flowing freely from his palm. Deciding now to abandon all caution he kicked off upwards, as fast as he could before the monster detected him.

His worst fears were confirmed. As he scrambled up the crater walls he heard a moan of blood lust from the prehistoric hunter. Luke transformed into human form, panting in fear as he clung to the ridges of the crater where it rose above the waves. The section of crater walls that rose above sea level were still so shallow that he feared the monster might still reach him. Looking out to the nearest land he saw an island about a mile away. It looked high enough to protect him from the dinosaur. Hurriedly Luke returned to Eeshu form and leapt off the crater edge and into the open sea. He struck out against the stormy water, desperate to reach land and safety.

Luke looked fearfully behind him. The dreaded form of the monster was snaking out over the submerged crater walls and heading towards him. Luke swam as hard and as fast as he could but it seemed hopeless. How could he out-swim that huge monster? Looking back once more he saw that the dinosaur had gained on him, its hideous jaws gaping to snatch at him.

Luke screamed for help and swum hopelessly onwards but it was too late. The monster reared back its long neck and lunged at him, trying to bite him in two. With lightning speed Luke managed to twist away and swim beneath the dinosaur itself, just in time to avoid the deadly jaws. The monster gave another moan of frustration, then swam smoothly around to make another lunge at Luke.

Luke realised that he was not going to be able to reach land before the monster attacked him again. Sobbing with despair he dived rapidly down, looking about for some kind of shelter below him, out of the monster's reach. With relief he spotted a deep crevice carved into the slope of a volcano. Luke swam towards it as fast as he could, all the time screaming in his mind for help. Where was Coryan, or Areeya, or the Wise Ones? The monster dived swiftly after him, snapping at his heels. This time its jagged teeth tore into Luke's foot. The pain of it shocked him into a burst of power. He dived into the narrow crevice, crouching as low as possible inside. He cowered in terror as the body of the beast darkened the water above him. The monster swooped around the crevice, scenting the blood trail from Luke's foot. Luke saw that several of his toes had been ripped off. He felt sick.

Without warning the reptilian face smashed at Luke's rocky shelter. It tore at the edges with its teeth in its hunger to devour him. Luke whimpered and huddled inside his disintegrating shelter, wondering why no Eeshu had answered his call for help. He wrapped his arms over his head, sobbing in despair.

There was a moment of silence. The monster had stopped smashing at the rock. Puzzled, Luke lowered his arms and peered fearfully over the side of the crevice. The monster was holding its head alert as if listening to something. Luke could feel the water shuddering. He realised the volcano was shaking. After a minute the shaking stopped.

The dinosaur swung its lethal head back towards its prey. Luke cringed helplessly, huddled as far down into his narrow rocky crevice as he could get. His foot was throbbing painfully. The loss of blood was making him feel weak. He braced himself for the attack but still nothing happened, so he peeped out over the destroyed edges of his shelter. There was a moment of stillness. Then the dinosaur made its final, deadly strike. With a terrifying shriek it raised its head and with open jaws gnawed savagely at the crevice. Some of its long teeth managed to hook the cord of Luke's bag. The dinosaur flicked its head and Luke was hauled out of his shelter. As he dangled from the monster's mouth he struggled to pull the cord away from his body. The cord snapped and Luke was temporarily released but even as he kicked away from the lethal jaws he realised that it would be impossible to swim away in time to save himself. He closed his eyes in defeat, awaiting the agonising death he had foreseen in his nightmare.

The water shuddered violently and the seabed began to tear apart. An unseen force suddenly dragged both Luke and the monster downwards at great speed towards the seabed at the root of the volcano. It happened so quickly that Luke scarcely had time to register what was happening. He heard the furious scream of the dinosaur as he tumbled out of reach of its jaws. The volcano shook and splintered apart. Rocks tumbled downwards into a pit of magma that had burst through the sea floor, sucking water down into it too. Luke looked around for the dinosaur but it was being crushed by falling rocks and shrieking in terror. Luke too was in danger of being crushed to death by falling rocks, or being roasted by the magma that was spewing out. He kicked upwards towards the surface but the pull of the water continued to drag him downwards. He wondered if he was to be crushed by rocks or burnt to death.

'It is not my time to die!' he shouted furiously in his mind but there was no reply. No-one came to help him or to rescue him. Instead he found the pressure that had dragged him downwards was now forcing him upwards to the surface at great speed. He could not comprehend what was happening to him. Then a chunk of rock crashed into his skull and the chaos around him faded into darkness.

It was the terrible pain that brought him back to consciousness. At first he could only register the pain in his head, his bones, his foot and every muscle in his body. He felt something touch his back and it stung him. His body began to shudder. He tried to open his eyes but it felt like too much effort. One side of his face was burning hot, the other side felt cool and scratchy. He tried to open his eyes again and through his lashes he could make out the brown knees of someone kneeling in the sand beside him. Am I on shore? he wondered. Yes, I can feel a breeze on my skin and my face is burning under the sun.

With a groan he tried to move but he could not even muster the strength to lift his head off the sand. Finally, he managed to turn his head a little. There was a blur of a face above him for a moment, peering at him but he could not see who it was as his eye lashes were so crusted with sand. With a groan he closed his eyes again. He was aware of voices shouting in a language he could not understand. They were repeating a word. It sounded like "Noura".

'I'm here. Over here, quickly.'

The voice belonged to a girl, but all Luke could see of her were the brown knees in the sand beside him. The girl stood up but he could not seem to move his head to look at her. Where am I? he wondered. He tried again to move, trying to push himself up off the sand and away from the burning sun but the effort made his head spin and blackness overcame him once more.

His next memory was of waking again, this time flat on his back in a bed. It was a long time since he had lain on cotton sheets and it felt strange against his skin. He struggled to open his eyes and a familiar face swam into view.

'Mum?' he rasped, struggling to use his voice which was harsh from thirst.

'Luke, my darling!' she sobbed and he felt her lips kissing him all over his face, her own face wet with tears.

'It's OK, Mum, I'm back. Are we at home?' he asked faintly, though speaking took such a great effort. He struggled to look around him.

'No my love, you're in a hospital in Morocco, though we don't know how you ended up on the beach here. They said there was some kind of small tsunami that washed you ashore, I don't know where from, and no other bodies were found. Oh my darling, everyone told us you must be dead, but somehow I always knew you were still alive.'

Luke sank back against the pillow, fighting off the blackness that threatened to overwhelm him again. He had so many questions to ask but he barely had the strength to say the most important thing of all,

'Where is Dad? Is he...OK?'

'Yes, yes, he's just sleeping. We've been taking turns sitting with you. You've been unconscious for two days now, and we didn't know when you would wake up.'

Luke tried to smile then fell back into the darkness. Only this time into the darkness came a flicker of white light. He felt himself leaving his body and floating high up towards this light and then he was surrounded in light. In front of him stood the towering form of Coryan.

'Coryan! What are you doing here? Where am I?'

'You are in a safe place. I wanted to speak with you, to prepare you before you resume your human life again. You still have your childhood to live, before you begin your work as the saviour of our oceans, of our planet. But never forget us, try to remember all you have learnt, and meditate as often as you can. You need to keep your connection with the Wise Ones strong and clear. In that way you will always be helped and guided in your task. I, too, will always be here for you, Luke.'

Coryan then began to recede into the whiteness. Luke called out anxiously to him,

'But Coryan, why would I forget you all, when I can be Eeshu and human? I can be part of both worlds, can't I?' But Coryan had disappeared from view.

Luke abruptly left the white light and returned to his body with a horrible jolt. He became aware of someone shaking him, calling his name.

'Mum, Dad?' Luke muttered, confused but aware of a feeling of panic, of some terrible truth that had not fully revealed itself to him.

'Wake up Luke, what's the matter? Have you remembered something?' It was his mum's voice.

Realisation made Luke sit bolt upright. With his mind he called urgently,

'Keeya! Keeya! Where are you? Keeya, I'm here with my

parents, but I don't know how I got here. Keeya!'

Nothing. Somehow the ease of communicating with his mind had been lost to him. He struggled to focus his mind on Keeya, sending his thoughts out to her. There was no reply. In his distress he called out aloud,

'Keeya! Answer me! Keeya!'

Then a terrible realisation dawned. Had his Eeshu abilities been lost forever? What had happened to him, between the volcanic eruption and his being washed ashore? Had his body been damaged in some way that it had destroyed the Eeshu part of him? Had he become wholly human again? Was his dual life as an Eeshu and a human being lost to him?

In desperation Luke tried to communicate with Keeya again but there was nothing, no voices in his head either from Keeya or from his friends of light. The grief of his loss overwhelmed him. In his despair he lost consciousness once more.

It took a week in hospital for his body to recover sufficiently to be able to go back home. Luke returned to Cornwall with his parents, back to the home that he had yearned to return to for so long. Now, however, it was the sea that he longed to return to, back to Keeya, Biblyan, Tiyan and Merya, back to the seals, the dolphins, the paradise island and all the wonders of the ocean. At times it all seemed like a dream and sometimes he even doubted it himself. When he had been in the hospital in Morocco, he had asked anxiously for his bag, for his crystals and his beautiful knife that Biblyan had given him. They would have been proof to himself and a tangible link with his Eeshu life. But no bag had been found. He knew that it must be lying deep at the bottom of the ocean with the monster, or perhaps even swallowed up by the fiery magma. Had that terrible monster been killed in the magma too? He desperately hoped so. Could it ever be killed?

But more pressing in his mind was the question of what had happened to his link with the Eeshu. All that remained of his Eeshu life was the strange ring on his finger, his Christmas gift from Keeya. Was it all a dream? What was real? His grief was very real. A grief that he could not explain to his anxious parents. They were still mystified by his disappearance and miraculous return, as were the journalists and television crews who flocked to their house, eager for the truth of what had happened to him. For a week he was a minor celebrity but his dull explanation of having amnesia and not knowing what had happened to him eventually made them lose interest in him.

He was still a boy though, with a child's resilience and ability to accept change and in the following days his grief softened into resignation. But he could never forget. Whenever possible he would visit the little cove where he had drowned and he would think of Keeya, of all the adventures they had shared, of the dangers and the laughter. He missed her so much. Why she had not tried to visit him here, or tried to contact him in some way?

It was almost two weeks since he had returned from Morocco. Luke was in the same little cove where it had all begun. He sat on the rocks, staring moodily into the restless sea, at the spot where he had been drowned. His mind would often return to his drowning. Who had drowned him? It was clear to him now that it had been the only way for him to enter the Eeshu world. He still wondered whether Coryan had done it but he could not bring himself to believe that Keeya would do such a thing. She would never lie to him. Had the Wise Ones drowned him? Would he ever find out? He had been so angry, so afraid when it had happened. Now he was grateful.

'Luke. Luke, listen to my voice.'

Luke froze, his heart pounding with excitement. Someone was calling his name, not out loud but as a voice inside his head.

'Hello, who is it? Is that you, Keeya?' Luke strained his eyes, searching the water for signs of his Eeshu friend. The voice grew stronger in his mind, calling his name. It was an unfamiliar voice, gentle and feminine. It was the voice of a woman. A strong, sweet perfume suddenly filled his nostrils. He looked around, perplexed. Who was it, calling to him? Try as he might, he could see no sign of anyone, on land or in the sea. The voice continued to tease him, whispering his name but revealing nothing.

'Who are you? What do you want?' he demanded angrily.

'Be patient Luke, this is not the end of your journey. You will learn more, very soon.'

The voice was now as clear as crystal. A pair of dark brown eyes appeared briefly in his mind.

'Noura will find you, and then a new journey of light will begin. Do not feel sad, enjoy the time with your family.'

'Who is Noura?' he asked impatiently. But the image of the dark eyes faded and the voice disappeared entirely.

Luke was confused. He felt sick with disappointment that the voice was not that of Keeya. But to have someone contact him telepathically gave him hope too. Who did that mysterious voice belong to? Was she a Wise One? Was she another Eeshu, watching him from out there in the bay? He scanned the sea in frustration but saw nothing but gulls swooping over the foam. And who is Noura? With a sigh, Luke gave one last wistful look at the sea and turned sadly towards home.

The story continues...

This excerpt is from the second book in the 'Light Travellers' series, entitled 'Noura's Journey'.

1
From Marrakech to Ouarzazate

Noura happily raised her face to the hot Morrocan sun. It radiated through a canopy of leaves with golden fingers of light. She sighed blissfully. She was alone at last, alone with her thoughts. Somewhere on the far side of the garden she could hear the murmur of her parents' voices but here in the quiet shadows she could lose herself completely in the magic. A week ago her life had changed forever and she wanted to relive the wonder of it all.

Even in the deep shade of the garden the hot, dry air of Marrakech was making her feel thirsty. Languidly she followed the sound of trickling water, keen to feel its coolness on her skin. Her thick, curly brown hair felt hot and heavy against her neck. She was so glad her mum and dad had brought her to this secluded garden, a green oasis within the dusty red-clay city of Marrakech. She felt weary after a busy day traipsing around the town. Even though this was supposed to be a family holiday, the main reason they had come to Morocco was so that her dad could take lots of photos. Her father, an English photographer, had been commissioned by the Moroccan tourist board to capture images of touristic interest. He had been granted special access to this garden whilst it was closed to the public. Her mother, a Moroccan by birth, was assisting her father in another part of the garden leaving Noura free to wander into the deep shade beneath the palms trees. Her mother had told her this lovely place was known as "La Majorelle" and that it had belonged to a famous French fashion designer. Noura was just thankful that she had such a heavenly place to sit and wait whilst her mum and dad finished their work.

Noura perched on an indigo-painted wall which

surrounded a large, square fish pond. A runnel of water trickled into this pond. She ran her wrists beneath this small stream before wiping wet fingers across her sticky forehead. She sighed with relief. Now she had cooled herself she could lose herself once more in her thoughts, her memories. Was it really only a week ago that it had happened? When reality and dreams had become one?

It had happened on a quiet beach near Agadir, a coastal resort where they had begun their holiday. She had been taking a solitary walk along the water's edge and had wandered far away from the main tourist area. Thinking she ought to turn back before her parents had noticed that she was missing, she spied a large object that was tangled in the seaweed just ahead of her. Thinking it was the corpse of a large fish or whale that had been washed ashore, Noura was astonished instead to find it was the body of a magical sea creature. Unable to believe her eyes she had crouched beside it, for it was laying face down in the sand, its limp body nudged by the waves. The skin of this creature was grey like a dolphin but it had the legs and arms of a human. The feet were webbed and one foot was badly damaged. The back of the creature's head was covered with matted dark hair. It had tatters of plastic around its body and its skin was marked with cuts and bruises. She knelt beside it and reached a tentative hand towards the creature's back, unsure if it was real, unsure if it was alive. The creature's skin had felt cold, rubbery and smooth. Her touch seemed to have awoken it for it began to moan in pain. At this point she should have called for help but something held her silent and motionless. Her head had become giddy and she had had the strangest sense of time standing still, the rest of the world dissolving away.

For more information about the Light Travellers series, visit www.lighttravellers.com

ABOUT THE AUTHOR

Alison Cooklin was born in 1971 in Colchester, Essex. After graduating in Modern Arabic Studies at Leeds University she spent the next eight years working for an Arabic speaking television station, which gave her the opportunity to discover the Middle East, its people and their cultures. Her visit to Morocco provided the inspiration for the setting of her second book in the Light Travellers series, Noura's Journey, where the heroine Noura faces a long and bewildering journey across the Sahara desert.

Alison then began a new career as a belly dance teacher and performer. It satisfied her creative energies for a while but the need to write became too strong and whilst her children were very small she began forming her ideas for the series of books that would become the Light Travellers series. Finally in 2015 her children's novel 'The Light Travellers: Luke's Journey' was published.

The author currently lives in Suffolk with her husband and two children.

16394491R00084

Printed in Great Britain
by Amazon